PRAISE FOR KEEP HER SWEET

'Sharp, shocking and savagely funny. Helen FitzGerald is a wonderfully original storyteller' Chris Whitaker

'A new novel from Helen FitzGerald is *always* a major event. *Keep Her Sweet* is magnificent' Mark Billingham

'I devoured *Keep Her Sweet* ... shite parenting and a dysfunctional sister relationship goes to fatal extremes' Erin Kelly

'Helen FitzGerald has an uncanny ability to balance savagery and hilarity ... an absolute banger of a book' Matt Wesolowski

'A wonderful book about a toxic family, funny, shocking and full of heart. FitzGerald at her coruscating best' Doug Johnstone

'A novel rippling with power and intensity. A true page-turner' Michael Wood

'At turns wickedly funny, breath-stealingly tense and utterly chilling ... a book you'll want to talk about' Miranda Dickinson

'Dark humour sings from the pages, and as shocked and emotionally bruised as you might find yourself, this darkness is balanced by unexpected moments of levity that often give you empathy for even the most unpleasant of her characters' Russel McLean

'Not for the faint-hearted, but definitely for those who love deadly dysfunctional families, whip-smart writing, and their stories dark, dark, deliciously dark. Love Helen's writing, always' Amanda Jennings

'A crazy but addictive, dark and funny read' Louise Beech

'The plot is ludicrous but in some way believable ... It's dark but somehow not. It takes us to terrible places and when we think we've escaped unscathed we're left with a sobering truth: that dreams and hopes and illusions about our lives may not be enough. And the ending: it's cathartic and it's satisfying. Something that a saccharine finish could never be' Café Thinking

'The strength of this book comes from the examination of family life. Of the spiralling madness and intensifying anger. Where both nothing and everything is happening all at the same time. It's a train wreck you just know is waiting to happen, and the only question is who, if anyone, will survive' Jen Med's Book Reviews

Also by Helen FitzGerald and available from Orenda Books

Worst Case Scenario

Ash Mountain

ABOUT THE AUTHOR

Helen FitzGerald is the bestselling author of twelve adult and young adult thrillers, including *The Donor* (2011) and *The Cry* (2013), which was longlisted for the Theakston's Old Peculier Crime Novel of the Year, and adapted as a major BBC drama. Her 2019 dark-comedy thriller *Worst Case Scenario* was a Book of the Year in the *Literary Review*, *Herald Scotland*, *Guardian* and *Daily Telegraph*, shortlisted for the Theakston's Old Peculier Crime Novel of the Year, and won the CrimeFest Last Laugh Award. Her latest title *Ash Mountain* was published in 2020. Helen worked as a criminal justice social worker for over fifteen years. She grew up in Victoria, Australia, and now lives in Glasgow with her husband. Follow Helen on Twitter @FitzHelen.

KEEP HER SWEET

HELEN FITZGERALD

**ORENDA
BOOKS**

Orenda Books
16 Carson Road
West Dulwich
London SE21 8HU
www.orendabooks.co.uk

First published in the United Kingdom by Orenda Books, 2022
Copyright © Helen FitzGerald, 2022

A catalogue record for this book is available from the British Library.

ISBN 978-1-914585-10-4
eISBN 978-1-914585-11-1

Typeset in Garamond by www.typesetter.org.uk

Printed and bound by CPI Group (UK) Ltd, Croydon CR0 4YY

For sales and distribution, please contact info@orendabooks.co.uk

KEEP HER SWEET

CHAPTER ONE

The Therapist

Unhappy families always cheered her up. Joy was smiling and she hadn't even met the Moloney-Singhs yet. She had walked past their house, though, hundreds of times, but had never noticed it really, even the engraving at the top: *JB Collins, ESTABLISHED 1895.* It was a bluestone fortress with bars on its meagre ground-floor windows, and was incongruous, sitting as it did between two detached verandaed weatherboards. Joy had Googled 'JB Collins' before the visit, thinking it the wrong address, but there was hardly anything online. Maybe it was originally used to store grain and groceries, like the infamous Pratt's on Mair Street. After the session she would get in touch with Anne McLean – no Frank Peters, at the historical society. One thing she did find online was the 'For Sale' advertisement from twelve months prior:

'Chic, romantic artist's retreat in converted nineteenth-century warehouse in the centre of historic and vibrant Ballarat, just a short walk to galleries, theatres, bars, parks, cafés, restaurants, shops and Lake Wendouree.'

The accompanying photographs showed a bright, minimalist interior with soft lighting and low, squidgy sofas. Joy was looking forward to getting inside – the outside was glum.

She had Googled the family too, as she always did nowadays, and wished she hadn't. She knew too much about the Moloney-Singhs to be fresh and non-judgemental – such as the fact that they lived in Preston for twenty years before moving here (and had perhaps overestimated the happiness 'architecture' would bring).

Second-born let her into the cavernous exposed-stone hall. Her name was Camille. She was polite and had a bruised nose. Joy knew from her mother's email that she had just finished studying English and theatre studies at the University of Melbourne and had moved home temporarily to save for her travels.

To Joy's surprise, the inside of the house looked nothing like the pictures she'd seen online. The lighting was stark and hurt her eyes. There were no squidgy sofas and there was stuff everywhere.

Camille led Joy to the other end of the hall and offered her a seat at the table.

'Your mum says you're planning to go backpacking,' Joy said. 'Where are you going?'

Before Camille could answer, First-Born pounced from a windowless room off the hall. Her name was Asha. She was almost identical to her younger sister except that every element that Joy could see was ever-so-slightly askew. She was twenty-four, and Joy knew from her mother's 'urgent' email that she usually stayed in Sunshine but had recently been placed on an electronic tag at 'our new (over-stretched!) house'.

Joy could see the contraption on Asha's ankle – it had been graffitied and signed, as if it was a plaster cast. There were scratch marks surrounding it. She looked like she hadn't been outside for a long time and could do with some broth.

'She's going backpacking in Werribee,' Asha said, slamming herself onto the chair opposite her little sister and knocking the table off balance. 'Six months rent-free and she's saved two hundred and thirty-seven dollars.'

'How do you know how much I've saved?' Camille asked, trying to remain polite.

The vibe was so toxic that Joy was positively beaming inside. Her family was not so bad. Her life was not so sad.

Camille eventually broke the silence. 'Mum and Dad are late back from hot yoga,' she said, without shifting her glare from her sister.

Joy couldn't look at the girls, so she took in the hall. Someone was trying to thrust a purpose on it, but she wasn't clear what. Photographic studio? Workshop? Art gallery? Retail space? There was a glittery dress on a mannequin, shelves with jewellery and pottery and candles on them, and galleries of paintings all over the stone walls. There were tags on almost everything in the room, including the upcycled table she was sitting at ($2,457).

'Everything in the house is for sale,' Camille said.

'Really?'

'My parents are setting up a "content house" – well that's this week's plan,' she said, waiting for Joy to understand. 'A "hype house", like the Tik Tok Mansion in LA but for Gen-X empty-nesters.'

'And in *Ballarat*,' Asha said, the word somehow scathing.

'Oh,' Joy said. (She would need to do some more Googling later.) 'What happened to your nose?' she asked Camille.

'Netball injury,' the girls said at exactly the same time.

The chemistry between them was making Joy's legs fidgety, so she resumed her scan of the space. She could smell stale coffee coming from the back end of the house. She couldn't see beyond the hall but knew from Google that it opened into a bright open-plan kitchen/living area with a huge mezzanine bedroom above. There were two rooms off the high-ceilinged hall she was sitting in: the windowless one Asha came out of, which had two single beds in it, and another with a high, barred window that was jam-packed with the most extraordinary array of objects: huge, steel pottery wheel right in the centre, desk, clay, piles of yellowing newspapers, sculpting tools, easel, clothes rack, paints, brushes, sewing machine, remnants, packing materials. If this was a memory game at a birthday party Joy would be winning. The chair she was sitting on was hard and rickety, and $355 was a crazy price for it, no matter what was painted on the seat (fifties housewife, holding a teacup).

Asha and Camille seemed to be having a staring competition across the table, and it was a relief when *Mum* and *Dad* arrived.

Mum's hair, and much of her hand-painted silk kaftan, were wet with sweat, which sprayed off her as she took her seat at the head of the table, exhaling as if she was exhausted with having to make feminist seating statements. Her name was Penny and she was fifty-four. Her email had sounded desperate. To do this visit today, Joy had actually rescheduled family number two – the McDonalds, whose third- and fourth-borns enjoyed driving like maniacs at 'hoon meets' and were in trouble with the law.

'My youngest, Camille, suggested I get in touch re family therapy,' *Mum's* email had read. 'After the girls left home, my husband and I moved here with such excitement, and it has turned into a living hell.'

Dad, Andeep, fifty-seven, could not decide which daughter to sit beside, finally choosing to shove a chair at the end next to his wife. Joy knew from Google that he was a successful stand-up comedian in the UK in the nineties, but made some kind of filthy blunder on live television and had moved to Melbourne to be near several other disgraced comedians. She also discovered online that Andeep had recently started teaching a stand-up comedy course at the Eureka Theatre in town.

'I hear you're setting up some kind of *contents* house?' she said to Andeep.

'Ha, *content*, well yes, the ideas are evolving all the time.'

She was a little shocked at his accent; she did not expect him to sound like Billy Connolly.

'Penny's an artist. She made everything here – that lamp, that was her, the shade anyway I think, yes, baby? Yes. All those paintings, that bowl – Not that one? Almost everything you can see. And I'm a comedian. We thought we could combine our skills.'

'Like they do on all those shows,' Penny said. 'You know: people are baking profiteroles or blowing glass, and someone's walking around telling jokes at them.'

From her tone, it didn't seem Penny had much confidence in the idea.

'The girls are going to help us set up a YouTube channel,' Andeep said.

'You haven't filmed anything yet,' Asha said.

'It's evolving' / 'It's a work in progress,' Penny and Andeep said.

Joy did the usual introduction about her experience and qualifications. She told them she'd lived in Victoria for forty-five years – despite her strong English accent – and was still working at seventy because she loved helping families work things out. She really did. It wasn't like relationship coun-selling, which Joy only dipped into when she was desperate for work. It never started with the question: 'Do you want to stay together?' Families don't ask that. Families are forever.

Spiel over, Joy asked them to take turns to say – in one or two sentences – why they were here. Penny didn't wait for the silence to get awkward:

'I think we're here because there are too many ideas in the house.'

Joy gave Penny a reassuring nod – there were no wrong answers – while marvelling that every idea in the space appeared to be hers.

After a brief pause, Andeep said, 'I think we're here because … Why I think we're here … One or two sentences…' He was thinking very hard. 'Okay, so I am starting to realise that it must be very difficult having a famous father.'

Andeep's wife and first-born, Asha, erupted into laughter. Asha choked on a sip of water.

Camille couldn't help smiling. It seemed to hurt her. She held her stomach.

Andeep tried to disappear into his chair.

'Asha?' Joy bit her lip. 'What about you, why do you think we're here?'

Asha calmed herself and took another sip of water: 'I think we're here because Camille made us come here.'

It really was so hot in that hall. Joy was finding it difficult to focus. 'Camille,' Joy said to the second-born, 'why do you think we're here?'

Camille took her time to think about it – she was very like her dad – then sat up even straighter than before, leaned in towards her older sister and said, 'I think we're here because she broke my fucking nose.'

CHAPTER TWO

The Mum

Penny was into therapy. CBT, for example (first and twelfth year of marriage); as well as psychotherapy (post baby blues with child number two); and marriage counselling (year twelve again, that was a tough time. Andeep had abandoned her to wail by his mother's death bed in Glasgow, for *seven* months). But this one, family therapy, had made her so nervous she did a vomit-swallow during the hot plank. She wished she'd never emailed the therapist and had only done so because Camille went on and on about it to her and Andeep, and she wanted to gain the upper hand. When they had marriage counselling, Andeep made the appointment, and the therapist was *so* on his side the whole way through. Penny exhaled. She definitely wasn't the bad guy this time. Also, the therapist was an older woman so might be more inclined to see through the lovable façade and see the true man who was her (all right, whatever) *lovable* husband. She stretched and breathed. The sessions might help her. But with what, her habit of point scoring? Penny had recognised it as an issue in CBT no.2 and had since done Very Well at not doing it. Perhaps she was terrified of being accused of poor parenting. This seemed unfair when she had done absolutely everything in her power to be a good parent all the way to the finishing line. She only ever worked part time, for example, right up till they left school. She had *wanted* to drop them off and pick them up and ferry them round and feed them food. She had wanted to read them stories at night and make mud pies with them and go to parent-teacher group and organise play dates. She had wanted to be a good mum, and she was. She had given herself over to it completely.

Sometimes she had to look through old photos to remind herself of all the above – and indeed there was a lot of evidence of her excellent parenting. There were so many photos of the meals she had made, for example. Andeep always insisted on snapping a shot of the table before they started eating, so there were hundreds of photos of picnics, barbecues, beautifully laid table after luscious food-filled table – in the garden in Preston, in the kitchen in Preston, in the holiday house in Portsea, in the tenement in Glasgow. In every photo she was smiling – a genuine beaming smile – because she loved hard work and she loved being a mother and she loved food. Penny added it up and estimated that she had made at least twenty-one thousand meals since having children. This meant she had probably smiled genuinely more than twenty-one thousand times, and therefore could again.

Andeep held her hand all the way home, a hold that had become more and more of a hand brake since they decided to create the perfect life. He was using all his energy to slow her down, and she was using all hers to pull him along this allegedly beautiful boulevard.

She had imagined this walk from yoga a great deal before the move, and they had walked a lot faster than this, and when Andeep stopped to chat to a friendly country local, he had said something really funny that she had never heard before. Penny had imagined a lot of things about Ballarat differently – much of her knowledge based on satellite view. She realised now that everything looked lovely in satellite.

Andeep pulled the hand brake on full to wave at Brendan Valencia from Mount Clear, who they had absolutely no time to talk to. Penny breathed in and zoned out, 'almost as if you're inhaling smack,' a counsellor with burgundy hair had said to her once; 'let everything go blurry.' She was really good at this now but could never do it for very long.

'And your third wish?' Andeep was saying to Brendan Valencia from Mount Clear in a genie voice that he had perfected in August 1990 and which had lost its zing in September of the same year. 'Tell me, what is your third wish?'

Penny squeezed his hand gently and looked at the time on her phone, but he did not take the hint. A good thing probably, because whenever she squeezed his hand like this, or kicked him under the table at a dinner party – despite lengthy discussions regarding secret codes beforehand – he would without fail loudly announce: 'Why'd you kick me under the table?' She didn't squeeze again – risky. She was Ballarat Penny now and she could listen to the rest of her partner's joke and work towards enjoying it. She would start with a fake smile. 'A fake smile might well turn into a real one,' a counsellor dressed in yellow had said to her once. The genie joke was a particularly long one though.

She'd never admitted it to Andeep, but when she saw him at The Comedy Lounge for the second time, she was devastated, and a little ashamed, that he was repeating the same routine. One-quarter of a joke in and she thought he was having a panic attack, why else was he being unspontaneously unfunny? As she'd only been to two live comedy shows previously, she didn't realise that, really, they were all just reading the same thing over and over. In her close-knit extended Irish family, repeating jokes was up there with being English. Andeep still told the same set of twelve jokes to this day, and it was difficult when people didn't understand why Penny did not laugh.

The joke wasn't over and she was late and vomitous. The children would be present at this counselling session – for the first time ever – and may say anything. *Children* – they were enormous adults, suddenly and indefinitely expecting her to make thousands and thousands of meals again.

If only they *were* still children – she would have been able to prep them for family therapy first. She would have been able to ask, bribe, no *tell,* them not to mention the time she ran away to the garage, for instance, when Twin-Pearls Janey had to break the window to wake her because Little Asha was playing teachers with Camille and punishing her with a fly swat. Andeep was at the Adelaide Fringe again at the time, an annual career essential that cost them four times what he ever made. Penny loved that garage. Apparently she had been asleep in it for five hours when Twin-Pearls clambered through the broken window and landed on her.

Brendan Valencia's laugh seemed genuine, Penny confirmed to Andeep, twice. Cheered, he eased the hand brake the rest of the way home.

Thankfully, the girls were so angry at each other that they didn't mention the garage incident, nor the time Penny smacked Camille for stealing her sister's favourite waistcoat then staining it with raspberry sauce then using green fairy liquid to completely destroy it almost as if on purpose. Penny wasn't in trouble in family therapy at all, particularly after Camille said the F-word. Mrs Salisbury recoiled and coughed, and paused for an uncomfortable amount of time. She was very old fashioned – Mrs Salisbury. She then went on about the importance of siblings, that they are your only shared historians, the longest relationships you will ever have and should therefore be nurtured forever like her relation-

ship with her beloved little sister, Rosie, even though she's
so far away…

Penny zoned out. She needed to call her big brother,
James, it had been way too long. She imagined him and little
Frankie wrestling on the gold lounge carpet in Coburg,
everyone laughing and taking bets, but never on Frankie.
Frankie was the youngest of the three boys (Penny's mum
stopped when she finally had a girl), and he always needled
and whined and picked fights – just like Camille – even
though he knew he would end up pinned down. It was like
he always wanted to play the victim. Penny smiled as she
recalled the rules of engagement for wrestling and other
games in her childhood home. James wrote them on the wall
of the treehouse one summer. She was so excited finally to
be included in their big-boy adventures. The rules were thus:

No weapons.

No groins.

No nipples. (Penny's idea.)

No heads.

Not on your birthday. (Frankie's idea.)

It was Frankie's twelfth birthday that day.

And James agreed … that this would be the rule 'from
tomorrow onwards'. Poor Frankie.

It made her smile, which was inappropriate, she realised,
as the table came into focus once more. The therapist was
talking about support and action and negative words. She

finally ended by giving everyone tasks to complete before the next session, some the same, some tailored. Great, exactly what Penny needed. Homework. Most of which stomped on her needs, like giving up her studio/office so the girls could have some space. This house had seemed perfect for the two of them, a groovy creative oasis with a workspace for each of them off the oversized and underused hall. It simply did not work for four people. Fine. She'd get her homework done quick smart, she decided, because it would be a good idea to give the girls some space. She and Andeep could visit poor Frankie in Laverton, or even James in Balwyn. No, a mini-break would be better, for everyone. When Mrs Salisbury finally left the building, Penny raced up to the mezzanine and eyed a five-star cottage overlooking marsupials and a creek in Hall's Gap. The girls would have the house to themselves for a couple of nights. To contribute – this was not an allocated task, by the way, the girls were not required by Mrs Salisbury to help in any way – to contribute, the girls could prepare the hall for the open house on Saturday and help with cocktails and receipts on the day. Such a good plan. Even if Penny only managed to sell the retro side-table, she would have covered the costs of this much-needed break. She had rescued the mid-century piece from a car-boot sale in Buninyong and was almost finished painting it gold. In fact $2,000 was stupid, she should be asking at least three. They could go after lunch. Before then she'd whip up a sexy black dress on the Singer. Hall's Gap, yay. You never know, Andeep might find some new material.

CHAPTER THREE

The Second-Born

I'm sposed to write down why it happened, the netball injury, and I'm having difficulty finding the beginning. It's just for me, so I know I can write anything, but it's a hard question, why. Even harder is when. Not last week when we did chest passes in the courtyard. Way before then. For inspiration I'm scrolling through our family group chat. It's illuminating; it's like a complete history of the Moloney-Singhs. Mum set it up six years ago when Asha left for uni in Sydney. For a few years it was lovely. We were all doing fun things and posting positive messages and funny gifs. I was missing Asha like mad but was also loving being alone with Mum and Dad. She got her time with them when she was little. It was my turn, and I milked it. We started going out for brunch on Sundays. Mum and I got into upcycling furniture. Dad took me to The Comedy Lounge once a month, and we watched movies every night on Netflix. And Asha was enjoying Sydney. She had a nice boyfriend for a while. Maybe she would have passed her final year if he hadn't ended it with her. That's when Asha became a stranger, when she returned from Sydney feeling like a total failure. She was not used to being a failure. If only she hadn't met that guy, if only she hadn't moved to that house of weirdos in Sunshine, if only that crazy church hadn't got hold of her. So many If Onlys. I am starting to think about Asha the way Mum talks about her little brother, Poor Frankie. Poor Asha.

Our group chat is called Nucular Family, which was kind of funny at the time but not now we're cooped up in this bunker. I'm shocked, reading over it. There has been a huge change in all of us, mostly in the last two weeks, but I can tell it started deteriorating three years ago when I left Preston to live the student life. Mum and Dad were on their own for the first time in twenty-three years. For a while Mum posted family photos every day, at least two a day, and we all felt and said the right things like 'aww' and 'ahh' and 'how cute are we', but after a while Dad stopped responding and Mum stopped posting. There was a lull till lockdown happened, then we all chatted heaps. I was living in North Carlton, Asha was in Sunshine, Mum and Dad in Preston. We sent recipes and TV suggestions and jokes and photos and links to TikToks and pictures of food and of things we were growing in our gardens. That tailed off after six months or so. Chat was now for important information only, like birthday dinner ideas and information about Mum's plan to semi-retire. She sent us links to crazy houses that they could buy outright: a houseboat on Lake Eildon, a converted tram plonked in a field near Seymour, a treehouse in Daylesford. (Guess it's lucky we're in this place and not on a houseboat – one or more of us would defo have drowned by now). Mum had itchy feet and was so excited. Dad didn't respond to the new-house ideas much. In fact, I'm just realising that he stopped posting altogether a year ago. He didn't even respond to our messages – not even a like or a love heart. Shit, he didn't even read them. His wee photo doesn't pop up at all. Not one time in twelve months. Can't believe I never noticed that. He just skedaddled, unofficially. I guess if he left the group officially we'd all see it in writing and it'd look way bad: 'Dad has left the Nucular Family.'

After Dad stopped reading, Mum stopped posting, except to put a love heart on every comment that Asha and I made. Just a heart, that was all. Looking at it now, it's obvious that Dad and Mum had both left the group. I miss Mum. She used to make beautiful roast dinners on Sunday. She used to take me to get my nails done. She used to find things funny. Now she watches true crime all day and drinks too much wine and looks like she just wants us all to go away.

I don't blame Mum and Dad for abandoning the family group chat, actually. Since Sunshine and lockdown, Asha had been sending prayers and hymns and links to church zooms. She was anti-vaccine too, till her boss gave her an ultimatum. She started spouting stuff about freedom that made the three of us very uncomfortable. Then there was the time I sent a message to Nucular Family that was intended for Mum only – something like: 'Are you going to let Asha go on like that? Bonkers. You need to step up and tell her off.' This sparked a separate thread between me and Asha that was not pretty and ended with us vowing never to discuss politics or religion again.

At that time, I set up a chat with Mum and Dad only, which I did not name and which we rarely used, not till I left uni and had to follow them here.

I wonder if other splinter groups formed at this time: did Asha set one up with Mum and Dad? Did Dad send messages just to Mum? Did Mum message Asha but not me?

No-one uses the family chat anymore. I messaged everyone to remind them about family therapy, but no-one messaged back. I think they've all muted it.

My stomach is sore. I wish I could put something on it, like Savlon or a bandage. Just gonna pop on a looser T-shirt, see if it works – hang on.

Sorry bout that.

So, when did it all start to go so wrong that I wound up with a broken nose? Last week? Three years ago? Or even earlier, like my eighth birthday? That's what comes to mind as the beginning. Maybe just because of what's going on with my stomach area. The loose top is not working. Gonna try a tight singlet then put a pillow on it.

That's a bit better I think.

My eighth, so she was eleven. Dad had been away in Glasgow for months. Mum had been spending a lot of time in bed or in the garage. Asha was taking me to school and back, stuff like that. She used to pack me lovely lunches, surprises wrapped in cling wrap, like roast-beef sandwiches and slices of apple. And she organised and presided over my party, which was wonderful right to the end. I invited my five best friends, played innocent girl games like pass the parcel and remember the things on the tray. We danced and ate fairy bread and no-one cried, not even Sarah who was the most sensitive of my friends. I remember Asha propped Mum up on the sofa, and she acted all parental when the adults dropped off and collected their daughters.

Maybe Asha was really tired after the party. So much work. She'd even made me a chocolate cake, which was gorgeous even if it didn't rise as much as she hoped it would. She got Mum to bed, and when she came back to the lounge she was different.

'Truth or dare,' she said.

'I don't want to play any more games,' I said. I was tired too. And I was watching something I liked on the telly.

'Oh go on, you start.'

'Truth or dare,' I said, still watching the telly.

She chose truth.

'Have you got a boyfriend?' I asked.

'Not yet,' she said, 'but there's a boy. Wes. I think about

him all the time. He's good at footy, I've watched but I don't think he knows I have. Nice hair if he used wax or maybe gel on it. Quite tall already, he'll go to six foot I reckon, his dad's tall. I know he likes me because he told his mate Georgie, who told Beth from netball. Now your turn, truth or dare?'

I also chose truth.

'Why do you hate your...'.

(I can't even write it down)

'...belly button?'

The question made me sick. I didn't know she knew it was a big deal, for a start. But mostly I didn't want to talk about you know what. I didn't answer her, and before I knew it she was sitting on me and pinning my arms down and lifting my party dress and squeezing toothpaste into my you know what.

I screamed. I couldn't breathe.

When she finished she got off and headed to her room. 'You need to grow up, Camille. It's ridiculous, you're eight now.'

I remember looking at my stomach area – there was toothpaste all the way in it, it was filled. The jaggy edge of the tube had scratched the inside of it and everywhere around.

I pulled my dress back down and put a pillow on top of my tummy and cried. I tried not to think about it – and after a few days, I almost managed.

Do you know what? I bet there's still some toothpaste down there, but I will never check.

There's a word for this kind of phobia, but I can't remember what it is. If I Google it, pictures come up and scare me away. I don't need to know the word for it anyway.

That's incident no.1, I'd say, which led to incident no.2:

It was my twenty-first. One month ago. Asha was living in Sunshine and seemingly on top of the world – a city girl, with a job, flatmates she adored and vice versa – even some new guy she was crazy about. To celebrate, she organised an action-packed girl's day out. She met me at Southern Cross Station and we hugged and giggled, so happy to see each other. We had brunch at Southbank, manicures in Collins Street and did some fabulous shopping in the Burke Street Mall (I got a white fluffy jumper, which I love). By late afternoon we were drinking cocktails on a roof in Lonsdale Street. And then tequila shots at a pub somewhere dodgy, can't remember where. We were heavily pissed by the time she took me to a secret location for my actual present, which she was so excited about. We had to walk arm in arm to stay upright, and we were singing. She stopped in a side street filled with independent shops and handed me a small gift. I hugged her. She had already given me so much. When I opened it I was so drunkenly in love with her sisterly generosity. It was a jewellery box. How sweet.

I opened the box and pondered. One large, gold, hoop

earring. Just one. I was about to remind her I don't have my ears done when she looked at my tummy and then at the shop we were standing in front of. Piercings.

Inebriation and fear came over me. She saw it, held my hands: 'You can do this, Cammy, you can do this. No more fear. I'll sit with you.' She took her flask out of her bag and said I should take a swig for courage, which I did. Which I fucking did, because I am an idiot and a fool.

Fifteen minutes later I exited that little shop with a piercing in my … Oh god, it is so hard writing this down. I don't want to. It's stupid writing things down. And this tight singlet is making it itch, I mustn't touch, scratch, oh god oh god.

I've had it for a month – four weeks! I don't know if it's infected or what, because I don't look at it. When I shower I only look up. I got used to doing this from the age of eight. Just let the water flow over it, and hope the toothpaste goes away.

Every time I think about taking it out I can't breathe so I don't think about that anymore. I just wear the right clothes and cover my tummy with a pillow or something if I can.

I'm going to change this top. It's tight, it's rubbing.

Yeah, I'd say that's the crux of it. Why netball happened.

ೞ

I'd been home several months when Asha gave me 'the present'. It had been quiet and nice. Mum and Dad were cool to be around; they were wanting to be happy. Then a couple of weeks after my birthday Asha turned up with a tag on her ankle, and everything changed. We all tried to be positive to begin with, signing her ankle tag and drawing wee pictures on it. We all felt so sorry for Poor Asha, for whom everything appeared to have gone wrong. But pity and positivity were overshadowed by Asha's anger and drinking, and by Mum's depression and drinking, and by Dad's constant absence even when he was present. If my thing is infected I reckon it happened the minute Asha walked in the door with that ankle tag on.

Camille Camille Camille Camille.

Sorry about that. Asha asked what I was writing that was making my face so slappable, so I upped the speed and intensity – I can write my name really fast, it's the thing I've written the most I spose.

The therapist said this would help but it's not. She's like the Queen of England: bright red lipstick, pointless and nearly dead. She didn't say what it might help with, and that's because I don't think The Queen knows anything.

You, Dear Diary, have been on my dresser since I was thirteen, stupid floral thing that you are. Asha pretended the tiny key must have gone missing when she was wrapping you – she went all manic making out like she was so upset;

screaming that it must have got mixed up with the expensive dotty paper she bought at Northland and which I shouldn't have torn because she was wanting to use it again for Anj McLean's sixteenth birthday party. I knew then she stole the key. I didn't try to find it, but I did keep you visible and accessible at all times and – as predicted – she has snooped regularly since. I know this because your first page is dog-eared and I haven't opened you for eight years.

Mum eventually agreed that family therapy was a good idea after the netball injury. She's always delegated to the professionals, and they have always backed her up, and that is exactly what happened. It took such courage to say what I said, finally out loud and in front of a non-Moloney-Singh, but no-one said a thing, not a thing. I rarely fight back with Asha and that's why: because I never win. 'I think we're here because she broke my fucking nose,' I said, and 'fucking' was all anyone heard even though swearing has always been an okay thing to do in this house. Not when The Queen of England is present, obvs, when she is present we have to pretend we all play polo.

I had to stop myself from bawling. I had to sit there and hold my shaking knees in place while The Queen set tasks that would help everyone but me, everyone but the girl with the broken nose.

Task no.1: move rooms, give 'Poor Asha' some space.

Task no.2: choose three family photos that depict happy

times and bring them to next week's session. (I am putting this off. I know it is going to get ugly. How, you wonder? Just you wait.)

Task no.3: is all about examining the 'netball injury' to ensure it does not happen again and I reckon I've nailed it – it all started when I was eight.

℘

It is true that we were doing passes in the courtyard and that this was consensual, even though I have no interest in improving my passes. I gave up netball when I was twelve, having given it a year. Mum and Dad were ecstatic dancing at Hanging Rock so it was up to me to look after Asha. I decided to exercise her like the rabid dog she is. An alcoholic one too – in the two weeks since she was forced by the court to live here I have bought her seven goon sacks of dry red. She was running out, and I didn't want to get her another one when she asked. She was already pretty drunk. She'd been messaging friends of Richard and had even made a fake Facebook profile, but she wasn't getting anywhere – everyone she knew and cared about was avoiding her. Even the house-mates she apparently adored so much, and vice versa, had refused to have her on the tag at their address – none of them were replying to her messages. Some mates. All this made her drink directly from the goon sack and beg me to buy more and pray loudly for hours, and I was going crazy. I know I know – why didn't I leave? Because she needed me. Because Mum and Dad asked me to look out for her. Also, why the fuck should I?

Eventually her prayers turned into songs, and that's when I made the fateful suggestion that we go out and get some exercise.

Asha was pretty good at netball. Before she dropped out of uni she was still playing once a week. As usual, she set the rules of our game, the most important one being that if you can't catch the pass, you must collect it yourself. I can now confirm that her chest passes are not chest passes but belly passes. And they are like cannon balls. I deflected the first two and – as per the rules, which at the time seemed fair enough – I collected the ball and returned it with as much accuracy and power as I could muster (not much). I got better at catching and throwing after a while, which seemed to rile her. Her throws became so hard and angry that they were almost hitting my tummy every time. Imagine, aiming for my *you know what* like this? I was able to catch still, which enraged her so much that she made a surprise move and aimed for my chest with as much power as she could. It caught me off guard and sent me to the ground. Doubled in agony I made my second fateful decision of the day. I stood up, collected the runaway ball, returned to my position opposite her in the courtyard and threw a lob so high that it went over her head, over the wooden fence and into the carpark.

I stood my ground. She had failed to catch it. She must now retrieve it.

We stared at each other for ages, the bad and the ugly. I raised my eyebrow. She raised hers. I might have smiled a tad. She pursed her lips so tightly they turned green.

'You know I can't get it,' she said.

If she left the courtyard her tag would beep, and she'd get arrested and hopefully jailed.

'A rule's a rule,' I said.

There was silence until someone in the carpark tossed the ball back over and it bounced between the two of us. We remained poised as if at a duel, watching each other as the ball's energy diminished. Eventually it rolled to a standstill at Asha's feet.

Next thing I know I'm on the ground and Asha's on top of me, actually sitting on my stomach, right on it, her legs pinning my arms, her eyes wild, the ball coming at me.

This was not a netball injury.

It is not a 'throw' if the ball is still in your hands.

❧

She's said sorry a few times since then, but she isn't, she just wants more wine, which I have so far refused to get for her.

We're in the middle of task no. 1 – moving rooms – and she just asked me again: 'Hey when you go to the shops how bout you get us ingredients for carbonara – I'll cook for us tonight, yeah, oh, and some wine?'

I said, 'No, Asha, wine's not good for you. It makes you angry.' This made her angry. She looks like she might jump on top of me again and actually punch me in the head with her bare fists – which is totally not allowed in this house, it's a rule – no ball this time, because I have outed her, you see. I have disgraced her, and she is Poor Asha, stuck in this house with a shackle on her ankle, without wine and without the love of Richard, who I prefer to call The Dick.

She told me she was in love the day of the piercing (how sad that my twenty-first will always be 'the day of the piercing' to me). Someone she met at that charismatic mega-church called 'Dance Said He'. She didn't tell me he was married. I didn't press for info, tbh, because I didn't want to hear about the church. I only found out after the court sent her here with an ankle bracelet.

We got drunk on her first night here and she told me all about her offence. I thought it was a really cool story at the time. Asha stood up for herself. Asha did not take any shit. Asha got revenge. The man she met at the church, The Dick, was married. Not only that, he was the pastor. Their love was incredible and they were soul mates. He had promised to leave his wife on the day it happened – it had been planned and agreed for weeks apparently – but he didn't turn up to their rendezvous in a Melbourne hotel. Upset and a little inebriated, Asha made her way to their church in Geelong, only to discover The Dick having drinks with his wife and several church elders. Asha stormed in and confronted him. He ignored her, he was weak, scared. She begged him. His wife told her to leave and said she was going to call the police. Asha told the wife she was wrinkly and grey and fat and ugly and bad in bed. The elders asked Asha to calm down. The Dick asked Asha to leave. Asha grabbed something from a nearby bench, walked right up to Richard and hit him with it. She then turned and left the building with her head held high.

After Asha relayed the story, I congratulated her – The Dick deserved it. Just how godly is a guy who cheats on his wife with a vulnerable twenty-four-year-old? We had a good night that night. I always felt really close to her when we were both hating someone else, when we had a shared enemy.

But now that she's broken my nose I'm not so into the story. The item she grabbed from a bench, willy nilly, was a coffee tamper, which is metal and heavy as fuck, could have killed The Dick. She was lucky to get off with a charge of serious assault and not attempted murder. The judge did not think it a cool story either, especially as she stalked and harassed The Dick and his wife between the offence and the sentencing, calling and texting and turning up at the house and the church. Asha was a hair's breadth away from a lengthy custodial sentence, and only avoided it because she had no priors and because Mum and Dad agreed to play prison guards here.

The tamper story gives me the same feeling as the school-disco story. I was eight and my frenemy, Rachel, said I looked stupid in my dress. I told my big sister, and she responded by riding her bike into Rachel on the way home the following afternoon. Rachel was quite badly hurt. She wore bandages on her knees for at least a week after and never looked me in the eye again. I was always proud of Asha for sticking up for me, especially with Dad away and Mum 'not feeling herself', but it did also make me a bit nauseous, a bit sad, a bit something. Same with the coffee tamper, now I'm thinking about it. That's two facial body parts she's injured recently.

I do mostly blame that church though. It's taken over the music industry and the government, and now it's taken Asha. They got her when she was weak – rejected, chucked, feeling a failure, working some shitty receptionist job in Sunshine, locked down with god-bothering strangers. Before she knew it she was speaking tongues. I can't wait to hear this btw. She says she hates sharing a room with me cos the tongues don't come. Sometimes at night I hear her chanting weird shit about someone called Nellie. 'Come to the light,

Nellie,' she says. Last night she was kneeling by the bed and swaying: 'Rise, rise, we want to see your beautiful eyes.' When she noticed I was awake and watching her, she stopped, embarrassed but not embarrassed enough, and got into bed. Mum and Dad, atheists like me, are calling it a phase. Another one: she's been having them since she was eleven, they're like the eastern suburbs.

Right now Asha's trying to hold it in, but she's not managing. She's folding her clothes very carefully – all seventeen items, five of which are actually mine, including and particularly the short, white, fluffy jumper she's shoving in her laundry basket right this—; my god she really has done it. I bought it on my birthday. With my money. I didn't even say she could borrow it. How can she stand there in the middle of what is now MY room, shoving my favourite jumper in her disgusting un-wipeable rattan laundry bag? She's almost finished packing, I'll be on my own again any moment.

It's going to get scarier without Mum and Dad here (can you believe they're about to bugger off, straight after our first family therapy session?). We're going to be on our own for three whole nights. Dunno why I think it'll be scarier without them here. They are useless these days, don't help at all, let her get away with murder. I must learn to hold it in. I will not say anything about the white fluffy jumper. Or my 'netball injury'. Or and especially about Richard.

It's like Asha knows what I'm writing – *Richard Richard*. Richard is a fuckwit, Richard is a conman. This pencil is fabulously scratchy. I'm going to use it from now on.

Asha is seething. She's probably written the word 'Richard' ten million times and knows the sound of it. I'm gonna check. *Richard Richard Richard*. Yep, she knows how Richard sounds. *Richard. Richard*. Ha. *Richard Richard*. She looks like she wants to kill me, but biological sisters don't do that, hardly any, unless they're practically men, royals for example. As far as I can tell, the sibling murder race goes something like this: brothers kill their sisters, and brothers kill their brothers, and sisters kill their brothers but they don't kill their sisters. I can only find two sororicide stories online – one involving care-giving, one involving Instagram. Maybe it's just we haven't heard about those ordinary sister killers, they're not documented, or they don't get inheritances and have nothing to scramble over, or they are too busy with their shared enemy (men) to hate on each other. Maybe they just don't happen. Right now, the last option is comforting.

Asha's taking the last of her stuff now – including and unbelievably my favourite mascara. Hold it in, Cammy, hold it in. I dunno, it's like a fizzing that gets fizzier as she gets closer to me, almost to the point of electrocution. Like last night – she prodded her forefinger into my arm really hard and said, 'Oi, can you message Richard for me?' (He has blocked her.) I believe I came very close to spontaneous combustion.

She's just taken my phone charger and I'm at five per cent. *Richard. Richard.* Richard does tongues and not just with Jesus. Richard is rich and drives fancy cars. Richard is calling the police. Richard is taking out a restraining order. Richard despises you. Richard is married.

She's popping in and out to wind me up, taking things that I need. The earphones, for example. They're noise-cancelling, they're MINE. Holy testicles, there must be a guitar next door – what was Mum thinking bringing that into the house? I can hardly breathe. She's tuning it, she's going to play it.

'Can I have my earphones back, please?' I yell, but she's probably got them on and doesn't answer and wait … here it comes … she's singing.

'Jesus, Oh Jesus, I am wild for you Jesus.'

The songs are all about Jesus these days, and I just can't bear it, it can't be real, it can't be that a relative of mine goes on like that, let alone that she seems to get all horny over it.

'Mmm, mmm, mmm Jesus.'

She says it like it's spelt Gee-suss. It's almost as if she's American.

She doesn't know how to tune a guitar and only knows four chords. This really is agony. It sounds like she is sucking Gee-suss's cock, deep-throating his lurve, give it to me Gee-suss, give it to me. Her voice is powdery and pitch perfect with no real feeling or emotion, and I am definitely on the verge of exploding. It is becoming clear, Dear D, that I need to do some deep breathing.

She's been next door a while now, but it's not over, she will be back. She didn't realise the 'retro' (= doesn't work) pottery wheel sits on a metal base that is screwed to the centre of the floor next door, so funny. She bagged the room with the window immediately, and of course I didn't rock the boat. They've been trying to unscrew the gigantic masonry screws for ages, but they've only come out a bit. Now she's smashing at the screws with a hammer or something, and Dad is wondering what tool he might need to borrow from Mr Valencia from Mount Clear, or if he needs a handyman. Asha's yelling, 'MUM,' but Mum's upcycling in the mezzanine. Dad's saying he really should go see if she needs his help with the mid-century 'piece' otherwise this mini-break to Hall's Gap will need to be a bank-break. Now Asha's making him take all his old *Glasgow Herald* newspapers out of the room, and he's huffing and puffing and piling them right outside my door, which is a total fire hazard, but I will not say anything.

Asha will come in any second, I bet, and suggest, all nicey nicey, that we swap rooms, making out that it will be a good thing for me to take the one with the pottery wheel. My plan is to complain but eventually agree, as if I am unaware that the wheel leaves no room for a bed. I don't need a bed in there. I can take the old gym mat Mum and I rescued from behind St Pat's and covered with faux sheepskin. It's really comfy. And I've always fancied a shot at that pottery wheel. I might whip up a jug or two for the open house on Saturday. Could be fun.

'STOP THAT WRITING!'

Seriously, that's what Asha just screamed. She's praying as close as she can get to me on the other side of the paper-thin dividing wall. She's hoping to get into the zone so she can speak tongues at long last, after all the stage fright she got from sharing with me. Must be like peeing. I am dying to hear her speak tongues. I am going to record it on my phone, such a load of bullshit.

'Shut up with that scribbling!'

She just yelled at me again, and I did well, I did not respond. She's in court again in a week. Her lawyer says they'll remove her ankle tag and put her on probation or community service, or give her a fine or something, and she'll be free to go back to Sunshine with all her Gee-suss-shagging non-mates. One week. Actually, six days and some hours.

'I'm trying to pray for fuck's sake!'

Seriously? I hate her. I hate her I hate her I hate her, she is the horriblest person I know. RICHARD!

What I should do is move across to the other bed, even if

it is still officially her bed, put as much space between us as possible. Right, that's what I'll do.

She's singing very loudly now, she's ecstatic, wouldn't be surprised if she has to stop the song for a moment soon. So gross. I can't listen. I need to get out of this house.

I guess I'm lucky I can.

You are helping btw, DD. Maybe The Queen's not as idiotic as she seems. More later, I'm off to the shops to get a quiet pen.

CHAPTER FOUR

The Therapist

'Seventy-one today, seventy-one today,' Joy said, blowing out the candle on the cupcake she'd bought herself. 'I've got the key to the door. Not for much longer.' She levered herself from the dining-room table Bertie surprised her with on her thirty-third birthday – instead of the mystery weekend away (to Rottnest Island) that she had regularly requested. She was saying farewell to the table this evening, along with many other non-essentials, not that there was much left. Most of her wedding crockery had been collected, and she had finally let go of her anger that Mrs Innes did not require soup bowls or teacups or saucers which had totally devalued the set. Since selling the house, she had done all her sobbing and reminiscing. She had filled an old-fashioned tartan photo album with memories of her happy family home: of Christmases spent opening presents in the living room and eating ham on the patio; of Jeanie celebrating her birthdays in the dining room, she and her little friends smiling like crazy; of she and Bertie playing Scrabble in the kitchen, reading papers on Sunday morning, having friends over for dinner parties. Saying goodbye to the house felt like saying goodbye to Bertie all over again. She loved Bertie, was even in love with Bertie, for forty-five years, all the way up till his death two years ago.

She met him during her 'big trip' with Rosie. Post uni, the sisters had set off on an adventure together. One evening, they became a little tipsy and started chatting to a group of dentists in a Melbourne bar. Joy never went home. She waved Rosie off and became Dental Nurse Joy for many years: dressed in white, her teeth perfect and polished, holding all the right tools, knowing all the right codes.

'3MOD,' Bertie would say, and she would hand him the correct implement and take note on his dental pad.

'ULBT,' he would say, and she would pretend to take note, knowing this secret code meant: 'You look beautiful today.'

She was the best nurse he'd ever had, the most competent, the most efficient, the most energetic, always able to handle difficult jobs. After she had Jeanie, this did not change. He called her The Fixer right up till his death.

She hated that she still harboured some anger towards Bertie. It wasn't that his personality changed with illness – it took two weeks from cough to rattle, and he was in another building the whole time – or that she discovered dark things after his demise, like that Bertie had another family in Adelaide, or that he owed one of the McCartney boys a favour. Bertie hadn't done anything dramatic. He was just completely clueless. Bored with retirement, he put everything they had into a new mobile business and lost the lot. It was his stupidity that had knocked her for six.

Joy tossed the cupcake, checked her lipstick, sprayed her hair in place, then shut the door on her beautiful, Victorian weatherboard home in Lake Wendouree. The house and garden had been her pride and joy for forty-four years, but she was not sad to let it go. It had never quite managed to feel like home, and she always intended to leave it eventually. Not in this mood, though. She thought selling would be exciting and happy, the beginning of something, not the end. She walked down the drive, past the BMW, past the *SOLD* sign on the dry lawn, past the rose garden and the shrubbery and the rockery, and past Bertie's mobile dental van, which was parked on the street with a *For Sale* sign on its windscreen. *Salisbury's Mobile Dentist* was written on the back of the van. Joy reminded herself yet again that there was no point getting mad with a dead man and that she needed to buy paint at Bunnings. Both sides of the van were covered with a huge, smiling, white-toothed mouth – which seemed to be more off-putting to potential buyers than the enormous dental chair galvanised to the frame inside.

She would miss the leafy walk to town but reminded

herself that the drive from Sebastopol would probably be quite nice too, and that it would be a relief to have a brand-spanking-new unit with windows that opened all the way, as well as some new neighbours to talk to. Dear me, she was little glum this morning, and she didn't have any explosive families scheduled to buck her up. Today was all about packing for the move tomorrow. A walk round the lake would do her good beforehand, some air, some breathing, and perhaps a quickie at St Pat's. It was her main respite these days, walking the streets of this old gold-mining town, the same song playing over and over in her ears – 'Wayfaring Stranger', the Red Molly version, a country soundtrack that made her feet twang because she was going to return to the mother country, her country, and to her own sister, her dear, dear sister Rosie, who was not mean or selfish like the First-Born with the ankle tag, but *was* all the way over there, still dying to greet her with hugs and conversations and ideas and gorgeous infectious giggles. They were holidaying together again soon, she and Rosie. And the plan was they'd go house-hunting for Joy, something quaint and not too far from Rosie's place, maybe even in the same village. Joy needed Jeanie settled first, but it was a lovely dream they had together and it wasn't impossible. Rosie was always sending her pictures of properties that made Joy's heart sing. Pretty cottages with roses and ponds and impossibly perfect lawns. They were in harmony, she and Rosie, always had been, like the song she was listening to. It shouldn't have startled her, therefore, when her phone rang.

'Put the camera on,' Rosie said. 'I want to see your face.'

It took several wrong swipes before Joy managed.

'Hold it up, stop walking, find a seat somewhere, take your time.'

Rosie was very bossy and ever-energetic. *Why shouldn't everything be perfect?* – that was her motto – and Joy knew it was worth following her sister's directions. She found a bench overlooking the water, settled in.

'Hold the phone up. Up, higher. Ah, that's it, that's the little face I want to see. Hello!'

Rosie was sitting on her floodlit terrace with a cup of tea, a huge cake with burning candles on the table before her.

'You made me a cake?' No-one had made her a cake for – must be years. Had anyone bar her Mum and Rosie ever made her a cake?

'It's red velvet with real vanilla in the icing, and there's a gooey strawberry surprise in the middle.' She blew out the candles. 'Happy birthday to you.' She sang the whole thing.

'It's so beautiful, I love strawberry gooey surprises,' Joy said.

'How are you? All packed?'

'Almost.'

'And tomorrow you book the flight.' It wasn't a question.

'Soon as the funds clear,' Joy said.

They hadn't seen each other since Jeanie's divorce five years ago; the longest they'd gone without a fun-filled meet up. This particular reunion had been talked about since Bertie died – the lakeside accommodation decided on, activities planned. It was to be even more perfect than last time, and last time was at a five-star hotel in Yorkshire, the best fortnight of Joy's life.

'What toothpaste are you using?' Rosie said.

'Are they yellow?'

'I'd say yellow-*ing*. That lipstick doesn't help. Totally fixable. Just sending you the polish I use, it's good. And stick with plain gloss, you're too old and thin lipped for that red. So you'll ring me tomorrow?'

'Soon as I've booked.'

'There's a two-bed in my street, you should see it, Joy. It'd be perfect for you. How's Jeanie doing?' Rosie asked.

'Really well. Home on Monday.'

'That's good,' Rosie said, but she was worried, Joy could tell. It was best they didn't talk about Jeanie.

☙

Joy didn't have a toxic family like the Moloney-Singhs but she did have a daughter ravaged by toxins. Ice, they called it – which seemed terribly unfair on frozen water. Joy loved water in any form, longed for the never-ending drizzle of Hampshire, for lakes and rivers and canals that were full, and for taps you could leave running for the duration of a two-minute tooth brush without someone yelling at you. Ever since she married Bertie and made Australia her home, she fell asleep to memories of white Christmases; of being snowed in for days with her mum and dad and little sister, playing board games in front of the open fire and walking the dogs along crunchy country paths. She even yearned for the smell of steaming clothing on radiators and for jeans that never dried on the line outside. Even Ballarat, arguably the most wintery place on the continent – how the locals complained – was not cold or wet enough for Joy. But it was ice that had nearly killed her only child and the word was sinister now.

Poor Jeanie.

How shocking that she now prefaced her child's name this way. Before her addiction she had been chortling Jeanie, dancing Jeanie, beautiful Jeanie, loving Jeanie, clever Jeanie, hard-working Jeanie, married Jeanie, happily child-free Jeanie, strong-single Jeanie. Until two years ago, Joy had considered herself a tip-top parent with a fantastic and fulfilled child who would never be prefaced thus. She'd had no concerns about her girl at all. They had a constant and loving relationship. To the age of forty-one, Jeanie jogged and played tennis and had mates and went on holidays. She managed a thriving florist and was essential to the success of the annual begonia festival – everyone loved her, she was popular Jeanie. She even remained strong and positive after her husband left her for more fertile ground – this was three years prior to Bertie's death and seemed to be more of a blow to Joy than it was to her daughter, who happily exclaimed thereafter that she had never wanted children really, and had in fact sabotaged interminable pregnancy efforts, unbeknownst to her hitherto adoring partner. Joy didn't like to think about her ex son-in-law. She had thought he was a good man; that they were close; family. Turns out he was just another idiot, now the father of two mini idiots.

It wasn't the divorce but her father's unexpected departure that caused Jeanie to spiral. It seemed as if everything suddenly caught up with her, and she became very low. Although, according to Jeanie, it was a one-off incident rather than a spiral – one innocent trip to The Old Smithy to douse her sorrows with a moderate amount of gin and tonic, and one snap decision. That's all it took with Ice, allegedly: one puff of a glass pipe. As Jeanie was suffering from grief and some kind of mid-life depression, she was enticed to take a puff. It was done without thinking. It got her when she was weak. It seemed to Joy that people were enticed to the drug for all sorts of reasons, but the reason they all kept using was exactly the same. The Old Smithy had always frightened Joy – she found it rough and dangerous, filled with drunk, uncouth locals calling women names. But now there was another group in the pub, not just the young men looking for dirty sex with scantily clad local girls, but motley crews of meth-heads, as they were known, staying up for days and terrorising the town. Even the unit in Sebastopol Joy bought had to be decontaminated before she could move in. Methamphetamine had seeped into the carpets and walls, and would have made her sick if she'd moved in straight away.

For the last two years Joy had watched her beautiful girl shrivel and rot. She stopped going to work and yoga, she lost her friends, lost her car, lost her house, her business, and her parents' life savings. Joy had remortgaged her Victorian home three times to pay for Jeanie's stints in rehab, before finally making the decision to downsize.

⁓

She headed straight for the confessional at St Pat's. 'Forgive me, father,' she said, 'it has been—'

'Four days,' Father Nigel said, his tone indicating that

Joy came a little too often. 'Honestly, Joy, you're seventy and you've never done anything wrong in your life.'

'Seventy-one,' Joy said.

'You're a good Catholic and a good citizen,' Father Nigel reminded her yet again, 'and there is nothing to be forgiven for.' He'd never met anyone with such moral strength, he continued: a staunch believer in family, a defender of the institution.

It's true about family. She would never have considered leaving Bertie, she had never needed to, she had promised to love him till death. She believed that divorce was wrong. (Jeanie, the MacManuses, even the Rossis. Whoever next?) She also had an unflinching conviction that parents who abandoned their children were morally bankrupt. Siblings abandoning siblings: what a thought.

'If you have anything to work on,' Father Nigel said, 'it's being judgemental. Not everyone is as firm a believer in family, as strong a Catholic, as you.'

It consoled her a little to hear all this again. 'But my tummy is all over the place today,' she said, 'and I just can't help thinking it might all be a little overwhelming for me, that I won't manage.'

Father Nigel reminded her that she was leaving the family home the following day, that her daughter would be moving in with her on Monday, and that the week ahead might well be one of the most stressful of her life.

'Go easy on yourself,' he said. 'After the move, don't rush around looking after Jeanie, do something nice for yourself. Can you do that for me, and five Our Fathers and five Hail Marys?'

Joy completed a decade – five Our Fathers and five Hail Marys was not enough for the lack of enthusiasm she had about Jeanie's third exit from rehab. A little less nauseous, she donned her earphones and walked to Bunning's to buy paint.

CHAPTER FIVE

The Mum

Penny should have insisted on driving. As per the rules she wished she hadn't made, the driver always got to choose the music, which meant she had endured the bang-bang-bang-banging of Andeep's eighties house mix all the way to Hall's Gap. Three hours and three-hundred M&Ms later and her head was beating too. On the way home she'd take the wheel and choose ballads. They might soothe and trick her into feeling something other than pain and irritation. It was 9pm when they arrived at the rental, a pretty stone cottage one kilometre from the village shops that was not as easy to find as promised. She and Andeep carried the suitcases to the veranda and fumbled in the dark for the lock. Once the door was finally open and the lights on, she raced to the bedroom, fully expecting her husband to follow her and pounce on the bed. Mini-breaks had always been so much fun. Time to themselves, no offspring; a clean house that they could mess up and leave; a comfy bed with fresh sheets. But Andeep didn't follow her. He stopped in the living room, went straight for the sofa and turned on the television, flicking through local channels and sighing.

'Fuck's sake,' he was saying. 'Even the ABC's all crackly. Hang on, hang on, there's Netflix – honey, they have Netflix. Hang on, fuck's sake,' he said. 'Password. It needs a password. Penny, is there an instruction book somewhere? Penny?'

Penny straightened the sheets she'd messed with her premature pounce and was now unpacking their two large suitcases into drawers and cupboards, and planning the rest of the evening in her head. They could go out for dinner in the village. No, there'd be nothing open now. Anyway, she wasn't hungry after stuffing her face with M&Ms on the way. She had a headache and stomach ache, and might make plain pasta with tomato later, or just have toast and vege. They could paint – she'd brought canvases and oils. No, that'd be better outside after the hike tomorrow, as was her plan for day one. They could ring the girls. No, that would put her in a worse mood. She was determined to feel close to Andeep again. Since the girls left their Preston home they'd become more and more distant. They didn't have fun together anymore. Empty-nest syndrome turned out to be a real thing. The move to Ballarat had done the opposite of helping. Andeep seemed to be out of the house most of the time since the move – joining this group, that group, running a course at the Eureka, making friends, having meetings. Add Asha and her ankle tag into the mix, and they hardly even talked to each other these days. Penny would sort it though. She would get her marriage back on track. She popped her head out the bedroom door. 'You want to have sex?' she said.

'Um, yeah, sure.' Andeep didn't look up. He was reading the information booklet he'd obviously managed to find himself and pressing buttons on the remote.

'Great,' she said. 'I'll go to the shop and get wine.'

ॐ

The store was closed, but the pub wasn't, and it was 11pm by the time Penny realised that it was 11pm. She and another drunk mother had been competing over who had it harder. The other mum was on her own with three boys (men, they were eighteen, twenty-three and twenty-six). The boys had not been invited on this mini-break but had come anyway. Within an hour all three were rat-arsed and throwing things at animals. Penny saw this and raised it: one home-wrecking, god-bothering, daughter on an electronic tag, one unemployed winder-upperer who was allowed to leave the house but never did, and one narcissistic husband who she didn't like much anymore and had to shag tonight. They were calling it a draw when Penny noticed the time. She ran home with a red-stained mouth and the plugged half-bottle she had left (out of the two she had bought). She fumbled with the lock for a while then screamed when Andeep suddenly opened it. 'You scared me,' she said.

'Sorry,' he said, making his way back to the couch to watch some dumb zombie show, not at all bothered, it seemed, that she had taken two hours to get the wine required for her to have sex with him. (She must not say this out loud.) She sat beside him and put her legs on his knees. 'I took two hours to get this wine,' she said, pleased to have left out the aggro part that was getting louder in her head. 'You didn't get worried?'

'I rang the pub and they said you were there,' he said, eyes on the zombies.

'Oh.' Penny tried to watch the television for a few minutes. She tried really hard, but it was so fucking stupid that she just couldn't do it any longer and went off to bed. If only she'd had time to whip up a sexy black dress on the Singer, like she planned. Mind you, why should she? He hadn't changed his T-shirt in three days.

༄

Every plan Penny made for the following two days turned to crap. Andeep twisted his ankle two hours into the five-hour Pinnacles loop and crawled back down the path, whining like a baby, blaming her in thickening Glaswegian the whole time (except when other hikers were within earshot. When others could hear he mustered allegedly witty one-liners that strangers laughed at).

'Why did you pick such a long and difficult walk?' he said when no-one could hear, and why didn't she pack his walking boots?

By the time they reached the house she was ready to divorce him, but she didn't say anything. She was determined for this mini-break to work. 'It might take a while to rekindle passion,' a life coach with no front teeth had said to her before the move to Ballarat. 'You must be patient.' But his life drawing of her on the patio in the afternoon was just plain mean. Her boobs were not saggy or irregular, and her nipples were not inverted, and her stomach was flat for a woman of her age and definitely didn't have stretch marks on it, not from where he was sitting, anyway, with his nasty, spiteful paintbrush. He seemed determined to wind her up, like he wanted to send her to the kitchen to finish off last night's wine before afternoon tea, and to the shops to buy more before they dressed to go out for dinner. At the restaurant he complained the whole time about his ankle, which wasn't swollen or bruised at all. The agonising crawl down the path had been for show, she was sure of it. And he feigned a hobble back from dinner too, both of them silent, hands disengaged. Back in the rental, he went straight for the zombies, and she went straight for the bed. She wasn't going to give up, though. Tomorrow would be better.

It wasn't. Her life drawing of him was also mean. Perhaps she should have eaten a good breakfast. And perhaps she shouldn't have suggested a perfunctory quickie after showering. 'No expectations, we don't have to enjoy it, we should just get our love muscles working again.' He didn't like this. He wanted *connection*.

'I'm not a prostitute,' he said.

Perhaps she shouldn't have said what man says no to a quick, no-frills fuck, and thrown her pants at him.

'You've made me really fat,' he said when she showed him her oil painting, which was no oil painting.

'Are you really fat or are you just really close?' she said, slamming the canvas on the outdoor table and heading off for a solo hike without a lazy, moaning man to hold her back.

When she returned, Andeep had finished the zombie series and moved on to an unhappy all-male Antarctica one. 'We've got work to do,' she said. 'Can you give the telly a rest for an hour?' Their account, as usual, was in overdraft, and they had to sell sell sell to survive another month. It was Andeep's job to write material for their first YouTube video, which they would do as soon as they got back the following day. In the video, she would bake Aunty Jane's famous brownie and wrap it in thick, hand-painted paper (they could charge seven bucks a pop at the open house, what with the original artwork on the wrapping and the careful rustic writing on the little cardboard tags and the twirly string and all). She left him on the deck to write his comedy routine, and she set up her brownie-wrapping materials on the dining-table inside. 'Don't show me what you've written,' she instructed. 'It'll be so much better if I'm surprised.' She set the clock for two hours so neither could slack off and tried not to look out the window at her husband, whose pen did not appear to be making contact with his new, essential and expensive moleskin pad, and whose eyes closed after twenty minutes. Penny didn't want to have sex with him, she didn't want to divorce him either. She wanted to kill him.

Thankfully, when the alarm rang, Andeep came inside and suggested they choose photographs for next week's therapy session. All four of them had been instructed to do this by the posh therapist with very thin lips. Penny was so pleased that he had initiated something. Andeep scrolled through the Nucular Family group chat. Penny had photographed and posted dozens of old pictures a few years back. She must have been feeling sentimental at the time because both girls had left home. She must have been sad, actually. But it was even sadder that she had stopped posting happy photos. She had stopped chatting to her clan altogether, she realised.

They both got mushy looking at the photos of their many wedding celebrations (registry office in Melbourne, family dinner in Lygon Street, drinks with mates at The Prince of Wales in St Kilda and a full-on party a month later at the Clutha in Glasgow). They found it difficult to choose three each, there were too many wonderful memories – when Penny carried baby Asha round the wreck that was to become their beloved suburban home, for example; when Camille and Asha both got bunny rabbits for Christmas; when they had that huge toga party for their fifteenth wedding anniversary. They laughed thinking about the wild sex they had after that party. Jess and Martin from round the corner got really pissed and suggested they swap partners. Penny and Andeep declined but talked about it in bed that night, a lot. They did used to have passion. They used to have sex all over that house, often outside too. Ah, the shot of the girls playing totem tennis in the blossoming garden; and of Camille's first day at school, Asha holding her little sister's hand to escort her into the building, promising to look out for her, ever the protector. And how could they leave out that first wonderful summer in Portsea, and the second and the third? They had at least ten exceptional summers in those golden years. They had been happy, quite often in fact, before the girls left home, both at the age of eighteen, excited to find themselves, never expecting they'd need to return.

After they'd finished with the photos, they made love on

the sofa for at least three minutes and smiled on the drive home while singing to Simon and Garfunkel. As they entered Ballarat, they were holding hands.

CHAPTER SIX

The Second-Born

We swapped rooms. I'm on a mat on the floor now. The pottery wheel's my bedside table. Loving the window btw, I can breathe, and there's an excellent place in here to hide stuff. Can't believe I found it. It's incredible, my best secret ever – she must never find you! The Queen asked us all to pick three happy family photos to take to the next session. She'd never have guessed that this might be dangerous, but I knew I had to choose very carefully, and I did. When I got back from town (with this silent, smooth ballpoint pen, plus ingredients for carbonara and the goon sack of red wine Asha requested) I did everything in my power to be careful, selecting three shots that I looked terrible in. I didn't damage the albums when I removed them, and I put them in a clean envelope to take to therapy, confident about my choices: two giggling toddlers on Grandma Moloney's swing, two energetic pre-teens at the Preston pool, two dolled-up teenagers at Wes McDowell's barbecue. My photo choices calmed me down, like the walk to town had, and I was happy when Asha came into my new pottery-wheeled bedroom, sentimental even, because I was remembering that we had nice times as children, mostly. Mum and/or Dad were around most of the time and stepped in if Asha lost her temper. Most of the time we looked out for each other, encouraged each other. Asha didn't believe in speaking in tongues back then, and she wasn't locked in a tiny house and didn't drink wine all day and didn't have a married ex-lover who hated her. Things were different. When Asha left to study at eighteen, I cried and cried. I couldn't imagine life without her. It's terrifying how things have changed.

'What do you think you're doing, ruining our old photo album?' Asha barged in and said.

Her tone alerted me to the danger immediately.

'I'll put them back later,' I told her, showing her the envelope and then the photos, which I thought would placate. She was always so pretty, Asha. I was always so proud of my big, beautiful, clever sister.

Alas – in the toddler photo Asha was chubby and I wasn't (she ripped up the photo and tossed it in the bin). In the pre-teen photo she had a bather's wedgie and I didn't (she scrunched it, missed the bin, then made a fist). And in the young-adult barbecue one I had sunglasses on and she didn't, which meant she was squinting and I wasn't (she ripped it up but held on to it, standing over my bed, closer and closer, her back stiff, her teeth clenched). I am so dumb choosing the one at Wes McDowell's barbecue. She'd fancied him for years and when he invited her she was so excited. We took hours getting her dolled up. But at some point during the event his best friend Henry Someone said something to Asha about me being a real looker. And Wes followed me around yapping about footy, he was so boring. Asha didn't talk to me for at least one week after that.

I definitely won't buy her red wine again – it goes the wrong way, like it does with Mum sometimes. Her voice changes and everyone is apparently out to get her, like me. I remained in the same position, lying on my gym mat, phone in hand, and suggested she go pray for a better personality. That was also the incorrect response. Her face went from red to white to grey. Her mouth area was green again. She began screaming that I was a selfish narcissist and a sponger and a blasphemer and that I was never going to be chosen, both her hands in fists now.

I may have asked why Gee-suss would choose an unwashed alcoholic criminal with bad skin and stupid hair, and before I knew it she threw the family album against the wall. The hard cover came off and the plastic-covered pages scattered. I was still lying on my faux sheepskin on the floor, determined to avoid another injury. Don't even sit up, Cammy, I was saying to myself, don't even look at her. I picked up my phone to scroll TikTok and before I knew it she was shaking and sobbing on the pottery wheel, and I was having strong impulses to press the peddle and watch her spin.

'You've ruined it,' she said, collecting the broken-off cover and the loose pages, and trying to put them back in the twisted spiral. 'Look, look what you've made me do.'

'I'm sorry,' I said, putting my phone down and sitting up. 'We can fix it. Hey, Asha, we can fix it. We can turn this round.'

She was weeping into her knees now, sobbing, breaking my heart. And as we collected the pages, confronted and moved by the happy faces of our past, I said, 'Let's have a mini-break too. From now till Saturday, let's have fun together. We can play music. We can make yummy food: carbonara and garlic bread, and salad with goats cheese and grapes. I bought it all, it's in the fridge. We can turn this round. Asha? I'm sorry. Let's have fun like we used to. We could set everything up for the Open House. Let's make lots of money so Mum and Dad aren't so worried and angry all the time. We can surprise them. Can we do that?'

❧

I made a lot of good decisions that night. I didn't use any negative words or even have any bad thoughts. The Queen would've been proud. I coaxed Asha into a bubble bath and unpacked Mum's record player. After setting it up in the kitchen we took turns DJing the daggy songs we snarled at as kids, with the volume so high we could sing full pelt without being embarrassed. It was so lovely to hear Asha sing something without Gee-suss in it. It helped that I drank wine with her too, after shaming her the way I did. I decided I should stop winding her up, be more empathetic. I matched her glass for glass as we fried pancetta and separated eggs and grated parmesan. Then we danced – *danced* – in the kitchen, in the lounge, in the courtyard, up the stairs and in Mum and Dad's mezzanine. We were Kate Bush, actually we were more like Mum when she's drunk, whisks as microphones, arms all over the place, all the wrong lyrics. The alcohol wasn't dangerous when it had somewhere to go and with food at the ready. I'm almost tearful thinking about it now. It was wonderful. I was high on my love for her. We ended up changing outfits three times and putting on green face masks, and I didn't mind at all that she wore my white fluffy jumper the third time and got avocado on it. Not a bit. Asha fell asleep on the sofa around midnight without praying or singing or telling someone called Nellie to rise, and I honestly thought about ripping you up, DD, after everything I've written in here. I was telling myself off big time for being a mean and horrible person.

Then she woke up. With a changed face.

'Will you do me a favour?' she said.

Fuckety shit. How was I supposed to say no after the evening we'd just had? 'Of course,' I said, nauseous.

'Can you text Richard for me?'

She'd asked me to do this a few times after court, when we were getting on okay, and I talked her out of it because she wasn't allowed to. This time I messaged him immediately, retyping as she perfected her words:

Hi Richard, Camille here (Asha's sister). Just to say she's doing really well and wants you to know she believes, more than ever, and will never give up. She is still praying really hard she knows it is working. She says she understands why you can't talk and that she forgives you and will wait for you.

~

I woke to Asha's finger prodding my chest.

'Oi!'

One day that poke and oi combo is going to cause me to have a massive heart attack. It nearly did this time, I swear, but I was still desperate to muster the empathetic Camille I'd been the previous night.

'Morning,' I said, rubbing my eyes enough to notice she had my phone.

'He hasn't messaged back,' she said.

'How did you get into my phone?'

'Your fingerprint,' she said. 'Wakey wakey, you need to make a Facebook page for the open house on Saturday and invite him. Don't you think, yeah?' She handed me my phone, fully expecting me to do it immediately. 'I've been up all night. Set everything up. It's amazing. It's going to be so good. We can make at least eleven grand, I reckon, and I can give a percentage to Dance Said He from my stuff. Mum and Dad are going to love me. I've done a spreadsheet. Come, get up, up.' She pulled the sheet off me, yanked me upright. 'We'll do the invites together. It's his wife stopping him, she checks his messages. But she won't stop him going to a fundraising event, she'll never even guess. I know him, he's dying to see me, this might be the way. Come, check out what I've done with the place.'

Asha had been very busy. She'd priced almost every item in our embarrassing shop-home – including, and unbelievably, all of the pictures and ornaments I bought on my school-leaver's trip to Bali, the roller skates I got for my twelfth birthday (and fully intended to use again one day), my prom dress (which I hated but wanted) and seven items of clothing that didn't fit me anymore (but would again after the two-week soup diet I was going to start any day now). I actually checked the cutlery drawer to see if the knives and forks had price tags, but she hadn't thought of that yet. She spent the day racing around with indignant huffing efficiency, moving furniture from one room to another then back again, cleaning walls and bathrooms and even my new bedroom, which she had no business doing. Thank god you were tucked away in my hiding place, DD.

'We can make beautiful jugs during the event,' she said.

'It'll add to the vibe: artistic authenticity. We've got plenty of clay, check it out, look, see how much clay we have? We just need to chop some wood for the kiln. It can make us money, Cam, yeah, are you with me, it'll be great, don't you think, Cam, don't you agree?'

'None of us can use that wheel,' I said. 'I'm not sure it even works. And we don't have a kiln.'

'We do. There's one of those small ones in the shed. Mum found it on Facebook.'

'Does any of it work though?'

She pressed the pedal and the wheel turned. 'Totally works, Camille. We can learn how to do this, we have time, why don't you chop some wood and check the kiln's a goer? We can charge people to have a go. That is such a good idea, don't you think?'

'Don't you think?' was up there with 'Oi'. It made my insides burn my outsides. There was no good way to respond.

She added $600 to the spreadsheet for the unmade pottery jugs ($75 each) and $1000 for the forty guests who'd defo have a go at it for twenty-five each.

She took photos of every item and put them on the Facebook page, checking each time to see who'd responded to the invite (no-one yet). She tried on outfits – all mine – she did her makeup – all mine – she drank, she put the wood I chopped into neat piles, then into neater ones. She lit and tested the kiln (goer). She swept the courtyard, watered the pots, put the awning down. She checked the Facebook Page (one yes: the middle-aged red-head from the Eureka Theatre). She did her makeup again, her hair again, she took selfies and posted them all over social. She videoed herself touring the house and put it on Tik Tok. She drank. She kept my phone in her pocket and checked it every few minutes. (Three maybes, none of them The Dick.) She drank.

Asha tried really hard to sleep that night but didn't manage and by Friday morning she was too depressed to prod me with her finger and stayed in bed all day. I spent Friday taking her soup and fruit and several fun, fizzy mocktails instead of the fresh goon sack of red wine she wanted me to get.

By Saturday morning, Asha's spreadsheet was looking very optimistic. So far, our open house was to be attended by three members of Sturt St neighbourhood watch, an elderly couple from across the road, the boss at ye olde goldy lolly shoppe, one longstanding member of the Ballarat Punjabi Society, someone from the Geelong Highland Games, Mum and Dad's hot yoga instructor (the yoga, not the instructor) and seven of my new local mates, including Spock and his bogan big brother, Big John. The Dick had still not responded to the invite. By the time I got back from the bottle shop with four goon sacks of red wine – 'for the guests, Camille, Mum said to get cocktails, they'll want a drink don't you think?' – most of the ninety people we invited had declined, including all our friends in Preston – I warned her that they never venture further than St Kilda – and all fifty-three members of Asha's church, including her Sunshine housemates.

It was dawning on Asha that she was being holy ghosted.

CHAPTER SEVEN

The Therapist

Moving wasn't as stressful as everyone said it would be – certainly not as difficult as Bertie's death, and nowhere near as hard as Jeanie lately – but once Joy was ensconced in her tiny cupboard-house in the altogether less congenial Sebastopol, she realised she did not know how and when it had all happened: how she had sorted and packed all her own clothes and belongings, taken Bertie's suits to the charity shop, visited Jeanie's rehab for a pre-discharge meeting, arranged and filled a skip and sold what was left of her crockery to Anne MacLean from the historical society – oh dear, she had forgotten to ask about the origins of the bluestone fortress that was home to family number nine. Over her first cup of tea in the low-ceilinged beige kitchen/living area, she made a note to do this on Monday, after collecting Jeanie, and before her afternoon sessions with families number three and five, both of which were certain to lift her spirits. There was terminal bowel cancer and infidelity in number three, and number five was dealing with a second suicide, yet both were determined to get though it as a team.

Somehow that day she'd also managed to take most of her trinkets and leftover antiques to young Ciorstan McDaid, who sold such things at the Sunday market and could do with the cash, as well as signing documents with the lawyer and collecting keys at the estate agent's. Finally, she had transported the BMW to her new unit, taken a taxi back to Lake Wendouree to collect the still-unsold (and unpainted) mobile dental van, and said a final goodbye to her old life. She had brought an extra hanky in anticipation, but the empty rooms did not stir her. She didn't look out the back windows, over the plum and lemon trees before leaving, and she kept her eyes on the ground as she walked to the iron gate and closed it.

To her surprise, the van started straight away, and she did not feel scared at the wheel. She had done it, somehow. Fixer Joy. She could do anything.

As she looked out at the flowerless courtyard in Sebastopol, she was relieved to get a text from number nine's second-born.

Camille here, it said. *We are having an open house this evening if you want to come? Beautiful homewares, pottery lessons, huge bargains, free wine. I've sent you a link to the Facebook page. Hope to see you there* ☺.

Joy had long stopped trying to separate her work and her private life. It wasn't possible in Ballarat. Already that day she had bumped into Federico of family number four, who was looking sober and might just get to see the kids next weekend. It was 4pm, so many hours still left in the day. She replied to Camille straight away: *I'd love to.*

Her Facebook Messenger beeped – Rosie: *How did it go? You get the ticket?*

What are you doing up at this time? Joy replied.

Waiting to hear from you! Did you get the ticket?

Joy hadn't forgotten. She'd driven the van past Nina Nguyen's travel agency in Lydiard Street, but there was nowhere to park, and it was closed anyway. Knowing these reasons would not be good enough for Rosie, she lied. *Nina Nguyen's onto it*, she said. *It'll be sorted first thing Monday. Can't wait.*

Rosie didn't reply. She might have fallen asleep. More likely she was annoyed. How many times over the last five years had Joy put this off? It was one thing after another. She added to her Monday list: *Go to Nina's.*

The local shops were just around the corner from her unit, but she didn't fancy crossing two busy roads. She didn't feel like listening to her favourite song over and over either. Today she wasn't a Wayfaring Stranger who was going home to see her sister. She was Sebastopol Joy. She chose to drive. She would try to be less of a snob; embrace her new community. In Sebastopol there was a bakery and a chemist and a Bunnings and a lovely Italian cafe. There was even a bank machine where she could withdraw her daily allowance of $50. She had no pension, not with Bertie's business venture starting up – as well as going under. Plus Jeanie's visits to rehab, of course. She must stay positive! The proceeds from the sale of the house, plus five therapy sessions a week, would give her enough to survive thirteen years if she stuck to the budget. She owned the unit outright, so she had no mortgage. She owned the dental van, and the BMW. She was in a good position compared to a lot of people she knew. Joy was good at sticking to budgets, and thirteen years was plenty. She was sure to die before then, everyone in her family did. Both parents (cancer), and all her aunts and uncles, bar Aunty Mary, who became the definition of a misery guts from eighty-five on. She didn't know anyone who lived beyond eighty-five and had a good time. If she had nothing at eighty-five – no house, no cash, no pension, no car – she'd just live in a cardboard box or – if she was lucky – in some kind of charity shelter and it wouldn't make her less happy than all the folk she knew over eighty-five. The only luxury on Joy's strict budget was her trip to see Rosie. It would be her last holiday trip to the UK. She would only go again to move there permanently. No-one her age really enjoyed holidays anymore. The Wilson's trip to New York sounded freezing, exhausting and extortionate. They had a lot of photos, but not one good anecdote. All they talked about was how happy they were to be home.

There was an excellent Aldi near the cash machine. Joy bought some essentials and everything she needed for the next few meals. Sebastopol was fine. She could live in Sebastopol if she had to, for thirteen years.

Milk, bread etcetera in her shopping bag, Joy returned to the cash machine and withdrew an extra $200. It had been a big week. She deserved to treat herself at the open house that night. Taking Father Nigel's advice, she had decided that the proceeds from the sale of the van would be earmarked on her budget for treats, and she'd always wanted to do pottery. That sounded fun. Back home, she unpacked her dressy slacks and pink mohair cardy and tried out her new walk-in shower.

Before heading out the door, Joy checked out the Facebook page for the open house, hoping scented candles might be on sale because her unit reeked of bleach and something else that she couldn't quite put her finger on. First-Born had posted pictures of herself in various outfits but always with the same pose – lips pouty, the same side of her face to the camera – holding home-made scented candles of all shapes and sizes, as well as oil burners, cute little bottles of eucalyptus and lavender, and painted pots with sticks poking out of them. Joy could afford at least two of the above, plus a shot with the clay on the pottery wheel. She looked for photos of homemade natural lip gloss but couldn't find any. Shame. Anyway, she liked her red lipstick. It made her feel good, it was her finishing touch. And Rosie wasn't right about everything. Joy never said so, but Rosie's hair really needed to be cut short. Long blonde had not worked for at least thirty-five years. She yawned. Two-days' budget for a couple of candles and some clay. She took off her heels. She had done so much that day, but she had not made up her bed. She decided to give the open house a miss and was about to unpack her linen when a video appeared on the page. It was the mum and the dad, Penny and Andeep, in the kitchen at the back of their bluestone fortress:

Penny is wearing a hand-painted floral apron and is standing behind the kitchen counter with a forced smile. There are several mismatched vintage bowls of ingredients laid out before her, as well as a glass of red wine. Beside her, holding a microphone, is Andeep.

ANDEEP
Welcome to our new You Tube channel, The Empty Claim. I'm Andeep Singh and I am a stand-up comedian.

PENNY
As you will tell from all the funny things he says.

ANDEEP
You might recognise me.

PENNY

Or you might not.

ANDEEP

And this is my beautiful wife, Penny, my most sensational other half, who shares this empty claim with me. She can make just about anything she sets her mind to, can Penny.

PENNY (forcing a smile)

Today I'm going to be making brownies.

ANDEEP

Today, she will be making brownies.

Penny adds butter and chocolate to a saucepan and stirs over a low heat.

ANDEEP

Mmm, butter, lots of lovely butter.

He is already struggling to commentate. The pauses are long, and Penny doesn't seem to have much to get on with bar stirring.

ANDEEP

My wife and I downsized to the beautiful city of Ballarat to live off the fat of our creative juices, and we decided to reach out to other parents like us who might be finding the empty-nest transition a little tougher than expected.

Penny stirs sugar and egg into the chocolate mixture. She waits for Andeep to explain what she is doing, but he doesn't. In the background one of the girls is yelling 'Mum!' It's Asha.

> ### PENNY
> *Because their adult children followed them.*

Oh dear, Joy was thinking, they should not be filming this now. They are not in good moods.

> ### ANDEEP *(laughing nervously)*
> *You might be wondering what on earth to do with your time now?*

Offscreen the yelling continues.

> ### ASHA *(off screen)*
> Mum! MUM!

Penny continues to stir the chocolate over the stove.

ANDEEP

You might be having trouble finding who you are as a couple again, perhaps you're struggling to identify things to do together, to find what you have in common, you might be having trouble rekindling your passion...

PENNY

You might be having trouble laughing.

ANDEEP

You might want to escape the rat race together, like we have? Perhaps you want to earn cash doing something fun.

PENNY

Perhaps you are terminally unemployable.

ANDEEP

Have you downsized to enjoy the goldmine that was your last property?

PENNY

Do you have no pension? Have you whittled away your piddly inheritance?

Penny takes the pan off the stove.

ANDEEP

Now it's just the two of you, you can reimagine your lives together!

PENNY *(looking directly at Andeep)*

Can you tell a joke?

Andeep thinks hard.

ANDEEP

Today my inimitable wife of twenty-nine years is making her family's famous brownie. Tell me, my beloved baker, where does this recipe come from?

Penny swigs the rest of her wine. Offscreen the yelling escalates.

ASHA *(off screen)*

Mum, seriously, Camille won't answer her phone. Mum! She's doing it on purpose. Mum!

PENNY

From my mum.

Penny sifts flour into the mixture and waits.

ANDEEP
And what are you doing now, honey bunch?

ASHA (*off screen*)
Where's your phone?

PENNY (*sweating with stress now*)
Nothing.

ANDEEP
What flour did you use, was it self-raising or plain?

AHSA (*off screen*)
Where's your phone? Maybe she'll answer if you call. Mum, Dad, where are your phones?

Penny ignores the commotion in the background and takes a deep breath. She rubs a baking tray with butter and waits for Andeep to say something. It takes a while.

ANDEEP
And now my cracking lover for life is rubbing a tray with butter.

A door slams. Another door slams. Penny mixes the chocolate, etcetera, with a dangerous-looking wooden spoon.

> ANDEEP
>
> *Looks like you just mix it all together in the bowl with a wooden spoon, as you will see my reason for living doing at this moment. She's mixing, she's mixing, such an excellent mixer, my missus. I did have a wooden spoon anecdote but I can't remember how it ends. So was that dark cocoa or, um, something different?*

> ASHA *(off screen, but much louder now, much closer)*
>
> *Fucks's sake, MUM!*

Penny grabs her phone from her apron pocket and throws it across the counter and over the screen.

> ASHA *(off screen, apparently catching it)*
>
> *Thank you.*

> ANDEEP
>
> *In a moment we'll be opening our doors for an open house – if you're nearby why not come and get creative with us over a glass of wine? There'll be homeware bargains and activities and...*

> PENNY
>
> *Comedy.*

Joy realised she was watching the video through her fingers.

There's an uncomfortable pause as Andeep watches Penny spooning the thick brown mixture onto the baking tray.

PENNY

You should have written a set in Hall's Gap.

Andeep scratches his head, thinking so hard. The wait is agonising as Penny continues plopping the brown mixture on the baking tray.

ANDEEP

It looks like poo.

PENNY (rolling her eyes at her husband)

Really?

ANDEEP

It does, it looks exactly like poo, it's just like little plops of turd.

Andeep giggles.

ANDEEP

Or, as we say in Scotland, jobbies. Wee jobbies!

He's really cracking up now.

Andeep's observation was correct and, despite herself, Joy found herself giggling too.

> PENNY *(not laughing)*
> *And then you cook it.*

Penny puts the tray in the oven, shuts the door and exits the set, leaving Andeep alone with his microphone. He leans in towards the camera and fiddles with some buttons.

> ANDEEP
> *How do you turn this off? Asha? Penny?*

Then he decides not to, settling himself behind the counter.

> ANDEEP
> *Have you heard the one about the genie and the guy with the big orange head?*

Joy grabbed her bag and headed out immediately. It looked like number nine might be needing her tonight.

CHAPTER EIGHT

The Mum

Her name was Vanessa. She had red hair and she worked at the Eureka. She was ugly but she was young. What Penny would give to be in her early forties. Vanessa, pfft. She had liked the YouTube video as soon as Andeep put it out of its misery – must have had a Google alert. Stalker. No wonder Andeep was so excited by it:

'Look, we have a like already,' he'd said, taking an unusual amount of time tweezing the spider legs that oozed from his nose.

Vanessa had knocked on the door at five past seven, the first to arrive. So brazen, with her healthy hair and her polka-dot dress. She had been the second last to leave.

Andeep, he was the last.

Andeep met Vanessa when he started teaching stand-up courses at the Eureka. Since then they'd had *meetings*. But Andeep always had meetings, ever since Penny met him that's all he ever seemed to have. Usually nothing came of them, and Penny rarely listened to the debriefs, because this is what they were like:

'This is top secret but X's friend X has slate funding and

is looking for a comedian to present a docuseries about X, and guess who's at the top of the list – well it's X – but I don't think there's any way she'll be available because she's doing X with Netflix and that's going to take ages. This really is top, top secret – guess who X's second choice is – ME. Also – and you cannot tell anyone, you have got to promise, do you promise…?'

(Who would she tell? What would she tell them?)

'…but it looks like X is going to give the green light if X is on board as director, and he's reading the outline this weekend!'

Penny wracked her brain for details. Andeep may have said Vanessa was planning a gig at the Eureka Theatre. A tour, maybe. He may have told her that Vanessa was a big fan. Pfft.

But Penny and Andeep had made love in Hall's Gap, they had *connected*. The drive home was the happiest she'd been since they left the city. When they arrived home, they were both overwhelmed at the work their daughters had put into the house. They had turned it into a gleaming, money-making machine. Penny and Andeep had rushed upstairs and giggled and whispered like old times:

I love our daughters.

We have done so well.

Can you believe what they've done for us?

Asha is such a hard worker.

Camille is so kind.

We are the best parents in the world.

The proof's in the pudding!

Penny was so happy that she had ignored the fresh bills on her desk. She wasn't even bothered by the rejection emails for her latest job applications (admin worker at the local health centre, assistant at after-school care, ten hours a week at a sandwich shop in the mall). There was a plan. There was hope. Hell, she didn't even care that Asha intended to donate some of the proceeds to her church.

They should never have left the city. She'd be a better wife and mother if they were still in Preston. There'd be enough room, for one thing. There'd be Penny's old job at the deli; routine. How she missed having a reason to get up. She was so stupid to imagine the two of them as childless young lovers again, dumb to think a mortgage-free unit was the answer; that they could live off the proceeds of their beloved family home and just potter around all day in Balla-fucking-rat.

She'd made all the wrong decisions and now – *Vanessa.*

ભ

It started to go downhill just before they filmed the video. Around 5.10pm. No coincidence, she and Asha were both always very nervous about any kind of party. Penny hated being a host and had a history of drinking too much before guests arrived, and while Asha said she liked parties and always insisted on having elaborate ones, Penny couldn't think of a single birthday she didn't end up crying at. Penny was very sensitive to the mood changes of her oldest daughter. And they were both very sensitive to red wine. Sipping in the courtyard an hour and fifty minutes before filming was a bad idea.

Andeep was having the longest shower in the history of showering, and mother and daughter began fretting. They had a video to film before seven. It might be terrible, was it too risky to post it live? And what if no-one came to the event? What if they made no money? What if Camille didn't get her message to Richard like she promised? Where was Camille? By half-five they had poured a second wine and were pacing the hall.

Asha's mood changes were sudden and scary. Unfortunately Penny had never worked out how to deal with them and instead always seemed to match them. At 5.45, Asha began setting up the tripod in the kitchen.

'It's nearly six hours since Camille left,' Asha said. 'It's odd, don't you think?' She was starting to get angry. No-one from Dance Said He had accepted the invite – she had hoped this was just because they were busy and she had been certain till now that Camille would message to say they were all on their way. 'What do you think is taking her so long?' she asked. 'Has she messaged you?'

'I'm sure she'll arrive with a carload of pals any moment,' Andeep said, finally showered and dressed and – in hindsight – looking unusually dapper.

'Do you have her location on that app?' Asha asked.

They didn't. At some point, Camille had turned it off.

'I'm just going to ring again then I'll press record. You guys warm up.'

Penny didn't get why she was sticking with her religious friends when none of them had visited her since the offence. She didn't know much about what happened. All she knew was that Asha had fallen for a pastor whose wife did not understand him. When the wife found out, the guy dumped Asha, and she responded by very publicly hitting him with a coffee-flattening contraption. Before Asha arrived home with a tag on her ankle, Penny had no idea what a tamper was. She now knew it to be a very heavy thing. It would hurt a lot, which was good, he deserved it.

The video was running now, and Asha was pouring more wine, her back straightening the way it often did, her neck going stiff, her face completely changed.

Penny was hotting up too. She was sweating – oh no, was it showing? She would do this video, though. She and Andeep, they would do it together.

'You're live on the count of three,' Asha said. 'One, two…' and then she disappeared.

Asha started making a lot of noise out the back, eventually

coming in while they were on air. It was as if she'd forgotten everything they'd said and was sabotaging the plan and the hope. Glad for the whole thing to be over, Penny lay down in the mezzanine and closed her eyes, telling the black colour to go away and inviting the blue colour in, like the mindfulness coach with the gammy leg had suggested.

She felt better by 7pm and answered the door to her first guest with a huge fake smile.

'Hello,' the guest said, 'I'm Vanessa.'

CHAPTER NINE

The Second-Born

I did *not* want to go to Geelong, and I was mad at myself all the way there. I am weak and stupid and I never say no, I never tell Asha my real answer and my answer when she 'Oi'd' at noon and said: 'Hey, can you do me a favour?' Was NO. NO, I do not want to do you a favour, Asha, I do not want to go to Geelong on the train via fucking Sunshine. I do not want to walk to the daggy prayer meeting 'not far from the station' (IT WAS TWO MILES), I do not want to find The Dick and give him a message because 'I know him, he needs reassurance and support, it's the synod, the elders, it's a conspiracy – they're all stopping him getting back to me, don't you think, don't you reckon, oh never mind, you don't know, you couldn't possibly understand.' True, I did not understand and I did not think and I did not reckon.

But she always manages to get me to do things I don't want to do, and I somehow found myself spending MY MONEY on a two-hour ordeal that involved changing trains in Sunshine. When I finally got off I realised I was on that Life360 family location app. 'In case one of us gets stolen,' Dad had suggested a few months ago.

We'd just been watching the news, and a woman had been kidnapped nearby. The three of us agreed. (Asha was not on the app. She was in her own home in Sunshine at the time.) We'd never used it, really, unless one of us was out buying cake or something yummy and the others were starving. I didn't want Asha following my every move on Mum or Dad's phone, so I deactivated it in case I chickened out and had to make up a lie.

I had to walk for an hour in the beating-down sun to this iron shed in North Geelong that looked nothing like a church or community hall. I couldn't see anyone or hear any noise coming from inside, and assumed I had the wrong address. I was about to walk off, readying my excuses for Asha, when a woman in her thirties opened the door. She was beautiful and she welcomed me with such a bright smile that I couldn't help but go in. The interior was nothing like the outside. Much bigger, for a start, cavernous. It was cool and comfortable, the walls covered in murals of lush countryside and full blue lakes. They must have sound-proofed it too, because the music was loud. There was a stage at the front where several people were playing guitars and singing one of the Gee-suss songs I'd heard Asha sing back home. There were about thirty people of all ages singing along, some sitting, some dancing. It was all very relaxed. The thirtyish woman said she was Rowena. I told her my name, but it didn't seem to mean anything to her. She offered me tea, biscuits and a seat, and headed off somewhere. The tea was good, so were the biccies. I was so tired. But I was not going to get sucked into that happy-clappy weirdo crap. I just needed a bit of a breather, and it was relaxing there. No-one was yelling or swearing or stealing my stuff or coming up with dickwad schemes to pay the bills. I decided to gather my strength before completing the first favour, which was to find The Dick and pass on Asha's message. This was the message (I had to repeat it several times. She texted it to me as well):

Tell him I understand why he's not responding. Tell him I know he might not be able to come and see me. Tell him I'm praying hard. I'm not going to stop. I won't give up. Tell him I love him.

The second part of the favour was to ask her friends to the open house.

I asked her which friends; what were their names?

She said everyone at the meeting were her friends, which meant I had to ask everyone there to travel 80k to our mortifying domestic selling ordeal.

I told her this was very short notice.

She reminded me they'd all know about it from Facebook.

I said even evangelicals might have other plans for a Saturday night.

She said she doubted it, but just in case, sell it, Camille, make them want to come.

I said I'd do it. I promised.

I was wondering how to get the job done, when someone tapped my shoulder.

'Camille?' a man said in a kind voice. He was sitting beside me. He put his hand out to shake mine. 'I'm Richard.'

I didn't recognise him. There were some photos that I'd managed to find online, although every time I'd searched there were fewer and fewer. Someone was sweeping the internet clean, drowning dramas about The Dick out with music videos and happy stories. In the photos I'd found, he had a beard, looked completely different.

Asha told me he took himself off social media after the affair came out. Damage control, she said. Pastors weren't supposed to do that kind of thing. The affair was a huge scandal.

'Why,' I asked. 'Did you both want to have sex?'

'Yes,' she said.

'It's a cut above most religious institutions then,' I said, 'if no children were raped. Dance Said He should be proud if that's all the blokes at the top are doing wrong.'

'Honestly, Camille, you are disgusting.'

'You're the one who's been excommunicated,' I said.

The Dick's hairless face was pretty nice, gotta say. So was his voice.

'I'm sorry I haven't messaged you back,' he said. 'It's a difficult situation.'

The thirtyish-year-old woman who'd made me tea was suddenly sitting in the chair on the other side of me.

'I believe you've met my wife, Rowena,' Richard said.

I was sandwiched between the married couple my sister had tried to destroy. The blood rushed to my head. She had probably put rat poison in my tea. They were probably going to dismember me.

'We're so happy to meet you,' Rowena said.

'We really are,' said Richard.

Dunno why, but I believed them. I have to say they seemed like the most normal people I'd talked to in weeks. But there was no way I could pass on Asha's message with his wife present.

'I'm just here to ask Asha's friends to her party. She sent out invites but no-one's responded.'

An old guy came on stage and took out his guitar. It was like an open-mic night, people getting up and down. He was catchy. Almost everyone got to their feet for a dance. I stood but I didn't dance. They were not gonna get me, DD, I am not suck-in-able. He sang two numbers before we sat down again.

'Would it be okay for me to get up and tell everyone about it?' I asked.

'Asha's party?' said Richard.

Before I could answer, Rowena said, 'Sure.'

I did it Band Aid style, almost tripped on a stair racing up to the stage, almost knocked the mic stand over. 'Hi my name is Camille.' Felt like I should add 'and I'm an alcoholic'. I didn't. 'My sister Asha Moloney-Singh wants you all to know she's having a party in Ballarat tonight and would love for you all to come. I'll leave details on the board at the back. Thank you.'

I headed straight to the board at the back, wrote down the name of the Facebook Page, then turned round to wave goodbye to Rowena and Richard. Shutting the shed door behind me, I put my earphones in and started the long, hot walk to the station. The thought of going back to our Ballarat hell hole was eased by the fact that food would be there. I had no money and I was starving.

I'd made it half a block when Rowena and Richard caught up with me.

'Hey,' Richard said. 'We're not stalking you, promise – our house is right there.' He pointed two doors down.

'Why don't you come in?' Rowena said. 'We didn't really get to have a proper chat.'

'No pressure,' Richard added.

I was wondering if they'd feed me; betting they had posh bread and stuff. And if I went in, I might get a chance to read Richard Asha's message. Hungry enough to risk a poisoning, I said yes and followed them inside their picket-fenced weatherboard. So pretty, it had roses in the garden and an enclosed spa area at the side. They were defo gonna have decent food in the fridge.

Rowena was reading my mind, and began putting together a charcuterie of sourdough, olive ciabatta, different-coloured cherry tomatoes, Parma ham, dolcelatte, real butter. I stuffed my face.

The place was homely: flowers everywhere, colouring-in pads and pencils on a tiny school desk, a half-done child's jigsaw and bunny cup with cordial on the dining table. On the kitchen bench was a *Women's Weekly* birthday-cake book and wrapping paper and presents (a doll, a sticker book, a train). One of the living-room walls was filled with family photos: old rellies, their wedding, Rowena in hospital holding her baby, Rowena and Richard standing over the cutest toddler, her little mouth poised to blow out two lit candles on a multi-coloured train cake. I had no idea they had a child. I guess Asha never mentioned it because I'd rightly judge her for being even more of a prick. Imagine, wrecking a family like this.

'I'm going to make some lemonade,' Rowena said. 'How about we have it in the garden? You go out and grab a seat, Camille. We'll clear this up and bring it out in a sec.'

They probs wanted to talk about me. It was time for me to go. But I didn't want to. The loungers in the garden were under the shade of a huge tree and had cushions that were so comfortable. Lemonade was on its way. I could hear ice tinkling. I love that sound. I was so sleepy and comfortable that I told myself to get up immediately and leave, that this was creepy and I was probably about to be strangled. I am going to die here, I said to myself, closing my eyes.

When I woke the afternoon heat was easing. I rubbed the goosebumps on my arms, wondering where I was and then wondering where Richard and Rowena were.

As if reading my mind, Richard opened the dining-room door and came outside.

'She wakes,' he said, handing me the glass of lemonade I'd been dreaming about.

'Thank you. I am so sorry. This is embarrassing. What time is it?'

'Six-thirty.'

'What? Holy shit. Sorry, I just mean shit. I'm really late, I've got to go.'

Rowena hadn't come out yet. I could see her wrapping the doll present in the kitchen. This was my moment to fulfil part A of the most recent favour.

'Listen, before I go, Asha said to tell you something.' I looked at my phone, read it to him as fast as I could: '*I understand why he's not responding. Tell him I know he might not be able to come and see me. Tell him I'm praying hard. I'm not going to stop. I won't give up. Tell him I love him.*'

There must have been a different door to the garden, because Rowena was behind me.

'Shit,' I said.

Rowena smiled. 'Can you tell Asha…'

To fuck off? I was thinking. To kill herself? That I will kill her if she comes near me or my husband or my family ever again?

'Tell her we're glad she's praying, tell her not to stop believing. She shouldn't give up. God will never give up on her. But she needs to know it's not possible for us to be in touch with her, not just because of the affair, but also the assault.'

'I had ten stitches on my chin, see?' Richard showed me the scar. 'Actually, hon,' he said to his wife, 'I don't think it's a good idea for us to pass on a message. It wasn't easy getting the interdict – any communication at all isn't allowed. Apart from anything, it wouldn't look good for her in court if it came out.'

'Of course, scrap that. You do understand?' said Rowena.

I said I did, completely, and that I had to go. I was so late.

'You're exhausted, poor thing,' Rowena said. 'We're going to drive you.'

'No, no,' I said.

'Yes, yes,' said the two Rs.

✂

'Your daughter is so cute,' I said from the backseat of their Audi. I was looking for small talk and this seemed easy. 'Is she with a babysitter?' I didn't realise I could not have picked talk that was bigger than this.

Rowena put her hand on Richard's lap.

He rubbed it gently, his other hand on the wheel. 'She passed four months ago,' he said.

'Oh, no.' I was shocked, sad. 'I'm so sorry. I had no idea.'

'Brain tumour. She fought for three months. And we prayed so hard that she would get better. Asha came to our church just after she got sick. We were both weakened by it, very vulnerable,' Richard said.

I'd have questioned his over-use of the word 'we' if Rowena hadn't added:

'The tumour reduced in size, you know, at six weeks. It was our prayers, we were all praying so hard. I thought your sister was supporting us. Turns out she was fucking my husband. So many couples split up after the loss of a child. You blame each other, you see grief in each other's eyes. I understand why Richard sought comfort.'

Before today I didn't know they had a child at all, and from what I saw in their house I thought they had a living one with a birthday coming up.

'Nellie, she'll be three next week.'

Hang on. 'Her name was Nellie?' I felt bad using the word 'was'.

Rowena nodded. 'Asha didn't mention her?'

'No,' I said, not telling them the whole truth. Asha may not have mentioned her directly but she had said her name, many times. Yes, DD, *Nellie*. I'd heard her say it over and over when we shared a room, and a few times after, if I put my ear against the wall. In the middle of the night she would start off by praying like an ordinary crazy evangelical, then it'd turn into a chant about Nellie.

'Rise, Nellie, rise,' she'd say between some Gee-sussing. 'Come to the light, Nellie, we need your smiles, we need your giggles, we need to dance with you, we want to push you on the swing, we want to do jigsaws with you, see you play with Mr Potato Head once more, we need to hear your voice, Nellie, rise, rise up, come back to us.'

'She's actually buried over there,' Richard said. We were just passing Meredith Cemetery. I was so moved, I wanted to cry with them.

They explained everything to me as we drove, and now I do understand Asha. I understand completely. She is even crazier than I thought.

&

Women have conned themselves into believing the stupidest things when they're in love with a married man. They believe he'll leave his wife next weekend, for example, or next week, next month, next year, or when his wife's had the baby, or as soon as the kids start school, finish school, when he finds a better job, when the wife's through the chemo, when her work eases, when the housing market picks up, when he gets back from holiday, tonight baby, mmm right there, I'll tell her tonight, I promise. But I have never heard anything as stupid as what Asha talked herself into:

She believed Richard would leave Rowena as soon as Nellie rose from the dead.

According to The Dick – who I'm gonna call Richard from now on, because he's not the dick I thought he was; my sister is – anyway, according to him, she had it in her head that he'd leave his gorgeous wife, Rowena, when little Nellie was resurrected, and that this would only happen if she prayed hard enough. He was crying when he told me this. Rowena had tears in her eyes too. They both felt sorry for Asha. Richard had sinned, he had cheated on the love of his life, his partner, his best friend. But worst of all he had caused a young woman to lose her mind.

I was wondering how Asha saw it all happening. Would Nellie's little fingers pop out of her grave one dark night; would she walk around, zombie style? I was trying to find a way to ask how she actually saw it happening, and how she became so deluded, when they stopped the car.

'Hope you don't mind if we drop you here,' Richard said. We were two blocks from the house. 'Best if your sister doesn't see us.'

It was nearly eight. They both got out of the car and gave me a hug. Richard asked again if I would keep our conversation private, especially about Nellie. They didn't want such nonsense to be circulated again. It was very painful for them and very harmful to the church, took them ages to clear it off the internet. The elders were livid. Richard nearly lost his ministry. It was the last thing they needed – rumours that they believed in even worse things than grave-soaking.

'Which we do not believe in!' Richard said.

'Of course not,' said Rowena.

I had no idea what grave-soaking was, I'd have to look it up later. My mind was racing with the lies I'd have to make up. I am terrible at lies. And Asha was going to grill me. I'd been away eight hours.

As if reading my mind, Rowena said: 'Why don't you just tell Asha you met me briefly at the meeting, but not Richard. And that I didn't say I was his wife. Say you told everyone about the party, and then went to the beach and fell asleep or had a rest; a lot of it is true.'

I promised this and one other thing, that I would

message them later so they'd know I got home safe and sound.

'Maybe text my number this time,' Rowena said. 'I've just sent it to you.'

'We promise to answer this time,' Richard said.

'But don't let your sister see,' Rowena said.

'Maybe delete any messages after,' Richard said.

As I ran the two blocks to our house, I realised I now had a lot of secrets. It was almost as if I was the one having an affair, with both of them.

CHAPTER TEN

The Second-Born

I walked in the door at 8.10pm. There were only two guests so far and I could tell Mum was mortified. Dad was talking away in the kitchen with the red-head from the Eureka, and Mum was trying to show The Queen of England how to throw a jug on the pottery wheel. So far all she'd thrown were wet clumps of clay all over her face, all over her cardi, all over the walls and all over my faux sheepskin-covered gym mat.

Suddenly, red-eyed Asha appeared from her bedroom door – 'Camille, in here,' she said, grabbing my arm and pulling me in. 'What happened,' she said, not letting go – she was holding my arm ransom. 'Where is everyone? Did you speak to Richard? What did he say?'

I thought about wriggling free. Her grip was getting tighter the longer I paused, but an arm pull would make her definitely angry and probably suspicious.

'I went to the prayer meeting and I met a woman called Rowena.'

'Hang on, hang on,' she said. 'What? Stop right there and tell me properly. You met Rowena? At the prayer meeting?

Start from the beginning and do it in order. I want details. What do you mean you met Rowena?'

'You need to let go of my arm,' I said.

Asha let go of my arm. I shook her heat off it, took a step back. 'She gave me tea and biccies, and I asked her if she knew the pastor, Richard, and she said she didn't and walked off and didn't come back again. I asked a few other people, but they said Richard wasn't around. I got up on stage and told everyone about tonight, and I left details on the board at the back, but I guess none of them wanted to come, although maybe they will, I dunno, because I left straight away. I walked back to town, and I stopped at the beach to dip my toes in and paddle for a bit, and then I needed a rest and I fell asleep on the sand. Sorry, can you move out of the way? I need to get out of this room. I'm really thirsty.'

'Wait, wait wait wait: "Richard wasn't around", "a few other people". Go back. Really, Camille, are you trying to make me upset?' She took a breath, gestured for me to start over. 'So you're outside the hall…'

'More like a shed,' I said.

'Whatever. I know, I've been there, a lot, so you're outside it, what time is it?'

'I got the twelve-thirty train,' then back-tracked as I needed to add as many hours as possible to my story. 'Actually, not that one, I was late. The one-thirty, so the whole trip took yonks, I didn't take note of the time.' See what I mean? My lie was growing arms and legs already.

'If you got the twelve-thirty you got in at two-thirty-ish – did you walk?'

'Yes, I have blisters.' (What am I like? She'd better not check, as I don't.)

'So add an hour, that's three-thirty-ish, you got there about three-thirty.'

'Right.' I was never going to get away with this.

'Then what.'

'Then I went in.'

'You just went in or you knocked and someone let you in?'

'Yes.'

'Which?'

'I just went in.'

'No-one opened the door for you?'

'No, then I met a woman called Rowena.'

Asha fanned her face with her hand and sat on the bed. 'What does *met* mean?'

'It means ... fuck I don't know. This woman saw me come in, came up to me, introduced herself, I did the same. She seemed nice.' I added the last bit as she would never expect me to say this if I knew Rowena was Richard's wife, even if I thought it.

'She's Richard's wife,' she said.

Good one, I got away with it.

'Then what. So you're in the hall, Rowena has "disap-peared"' – she actually did air quotes – 'and you're standing there with a cup of tea.'

'Sitting.'

'Sitting with a cup of tea. Then what?'

I repeated the story about the tea and the biccies and Rowena walking off and disappearing, each step punctuated with a 'then what'.

'And you say you got up on stage and announced the party?'

'Yes.'

'You just got up on stage, willy nilly. Did someone say you could?'

'Yes. No.'

'Yes or no?'

'Both.'

'Why are you being cruel to me?'

'Yes, I got up on stage. No, I didn't get permission. I just did it. Everyone was getting up if they wanted, singing and stuff, it seemed okay.'

'What did you say exactly?'

'I said my name and that you're my sister, and that you're having a party tonight and wanted everyone to know they're invited, that you'd love to see them.'

'That's what you said? You made me sound desperate. Is that all you said?'

'Yeah.'

'You said you'd sell it, you promised you'd sell it.'

The room was starting to shudder like the insides of me.

'And then.'

'I put a note on the board with the Facebook page and left.'

'Uh-huh,' she said.

'And there was a bit of a wait for the next train, so I went to the waterfront … And I had a paddle cos it was hot and sat down for a bit. And I fell asleep on the sand.'

'Uh-huh.'

She had my backpack and was looking through it. Uh-oh.

'There's no sand anywhere. Take your runners off.'

'No.'

'Why not?'

'Why should I?'

She emptied my bag onto the mattress. 'There's no sun cream. Thirty degrees today. Asleep on the beach in the middle of the afternoon. You are not remotely sunburnt. Are you? Where's the sunburn?'

She was grabbing my T-shirt, checking my shoulders.

'I sat in the shade.'

'You said you lay on the sand.'

Even Asha seemed bored with the direction her grilling was taking. She backtracked to the part that mattered.

'What did Rowena say to you exactly, tell me again. Was she in her mumsy wear? What was her skin looking like, splotchy? Did she have baggy eyes? Had she done her roots?'

'I didn't notice her roots. She said "Hi, I'm Rowena, nice to meet you," or something like that. Her skin looked fine to me.'

She nodded. 'Then what.'

Then what? Then what? Then what? Then what? 'Then nothing! I'm exhausted, leave me alone.'

'This is all BULLSHIT,' she said, 'you are telling me bullshit. There are holes everywhere, Camille, it's nearly eight-thirty. You left at noon.'

She licked her finger, swiped my ankle with it then licked it again. 'Not at all salty, and there's no free shade at the waterfront. You are lying. What were you doing? They got to you, didn't they? Rowena doing damage control, using me as a scapegoat. I know you know things, I can see it. Start again, it's 3.30pm, although that's probably a lie too, you probably got there much earlier. Start over, we're going through it again, you're outside the hall.'

'More like a shed,' I said, storming out of her bedroom and slamming the door.

I grabbed a glass of water from the kitchen and went out into the courtyard.

A few moments later, Asha came out too. I was terrified. But she walked straight past me to get her bike out of the shed. She wheeled it through the kitchen area and through the hall. I heard Mum yell, 'Asha, Ash, don't!', then the front door banged and the tag machine thingy in the kitchen started going *beep beep beep beep*. She was gone.

The cops came straight away and asked where she might have gone. The beeper only alerted them to her absence, it didn't tell them where she was. We guessed she might be cycling to Geelong, and they left to look for her.

Meanwhile the open house was getting busy but everyone looked really bored. Mum was plying everyone with wine, which meant it would probably go on forever. I messaged the friends of mine who I'd invited and told them, 'Whatever you do, do not come to this party. It is the worst ever!' Spock said a few of them were going out to Jimmy's club after the pubs closed. I told them I'd meet them there.

It was bliss with Asha gone, the most restful three hours at home since she moved back. Even with Mum and Dad obviously hating each other's guts. Even though the open house was the biggest bore ever – at this point it was up there with Asha's twelfth as the worst party I've been to (I bought her something she hated, a T-shirt from Victoria market. Okay, it was ill fitting, I didn't give it enough thought, didn't have any money, but there was no need for her to throw it in the bin in front of everyone). Even with the red-head rummaging through the mezzanine without permission and asking Mum how much for the life painting of Dad. Despite all that I could breathe properly at last. The curfew machine thingy in our kitchen beeped continuously the whole time she was gone, which you think would be annoying, but I loved the constant reminder that she was not inside the house and that she would soon be incarcerated someplace else. I'd even started writing a list of things to do – e.g., ask (again) for some shifts at Sovereign Hill, door knock at the local bars and cafes, find work, save money, get outta here! I stayed in Asha's room mostly, as the pottery wheel in my room was being used on and off. More locals came and went. I could hear Brendan Valencia from Mount Clear bargaining over the dining chairs Mum painted fifties style. Some guy from the Scottish Independence Movement was talking politics to Dad so loudly you'd think they were disagreeing, which they weren't.

I was about to go to Jimmy's to meet Spock. There were only two remaining guests at that point, and they looked like they might leave – *finally*. I came out of the room, surprised to see most of our furniture gone, when the doorbell rang. It was the two cops who'd come before. And Asha. And her bike.

Fuckety fuck.

That ankle tag obviously means nothing, it's as useless as the interdict Richard has out on her, which hasn't stopped her ringing and messaging and chasing him incessantly. Nothing stops her doing whatever she wants. All I can hope is they jail her after court next week. I am almost tempted to pray: 'Dear god, please lock up my sister forever, amen.'

They found her asleep in Meredith Cemetery. She told them she was on her way to Geelong and got tired, but I know why she was there. Nellie.

The cop with the glasses said he didn't think she'd get in trouble at court. He said the tag would be removed if she behaves herself from now on, that the judge will be sympathetic, considering. He said he felt so sorry for the poor thing when he found her like that. She was shivering, didn't have a jumper on, he said. She was covered in dirt and sobbing and talking gibberish. He assumed she was drunk. He had no idea she was speaking McTongues over some poor child's grave. She'd been behaving herself for two weeks, after all, the cop said. As long as she didn't leave the house at all before Friday she should be fine.

I didn't put him right. It was too embarrassing to say what she was really doing, although I'm really not sure what she was doing exactly, maybe she was digging the poor kid out. I must investigate. Also, I had promised never to mention the Rise Nellie thing and I'm good at promises.

Sidekick cop had sideburns to match and was less idiotic than the one with the glasses. He said they had to stop three times on the way back from Meredith so she could hurl on the side of the road and that she should behave herself and follow the orders of the court in future.

When the cops left, our two sorry guests – The Queen and the redhead – seemed to lose interest in leaving, nosy bastards, they wanted to stay on for the show. Dad suggested everyone should sit at the big table in the front hall for tea and brownies, but all the chairs were gone – Brendan Valencia from Mount Clear must have got a good price. So we stood around the table. Asha had a blanket around her and glared at me. No-one knew what to say, even when Dad came back with the tea. Eventually, my phone broke the silence. It was so loud. I didn't look at it. I turned it off.

'Who was that?' Asha said.

'Sorry?' I said.

This was an aggravating answer. Mum gave me a familiar look, I knew what it meant: *Don't wind her up, Camille.*

'That's your phone alert, I know the sound. Who just texted you?'

'I don't know,' I said. It was true. But dread was heating me up. I had forgotten to message the two Rs to say I got home safe. It was them. It was probably them.

'I'm off to Jimmy's,' I said. 'Spock and the others are waiting for me.' I made for the door.

'Why don't you look at the message first,' Asha said. 'It might be one of my friends.'

'Your friends don't know my phone number, they only have the Facebook invite,' I said. 'Bye everyone, I'm late,' I said, almost making it out the door.

Asha banged it shut, nearly got my finger.

'It's Richard, isn't it, or his piggy wife. Show me your phone.'

'Why would he message me?'

'Because you saw him today, for hours and hours.'

'I told you already. I didn't see him.' I was sticking to this lie, it was sensible. I tried to open the door again, but she held it firm. The Queen and the red-head from The Eureka looked frightened now. If they wanted to leave, they couldn't.

'Show me your phone,' she said.

'No, let me out.' I held my phone behind my back.

She was wondering how to grab it. She wouldn't hurt me in front of two strangers. Mind you, neither of them would give a shit. They'd both probably call it a 'phone injury'.

'Maybe you should go lie down for a bit,' I suggested, mortified. I didn't care about The Queen or the red-headed divorcee from The Eureka, even though she was totally flirting with my father, but I did not want them to keep witnessing the fuck-up that is my family.

'Thanks so much for the tea,' said The Queen. 'I think I'll head off now.'

At least she had some decency. She made her way to the door, which we were both blocking. I tried to move aside for her, but Asha would not budge. She had me barricaded against it.

The red-head was nervously eating a third piece of brownie.

'Perhaps a lie down would be a good idea, Asha,' said The Queen, trying to intervene. She had her keys and two scented candles in her hands, and a misshaped clay jug.

'I don't want to fucking lie down,' she said to The Queen. 'I want to know why my sister won't show me her message. It's him. I know it is. You saw him. I know you did. You left at midday, you got back at 8.10. What took you so long, what were you doing, what did he say to you, why is he texting you?'

'He is not texting me and I did not see him,' I said. 'I did see Gee-suss though.' I paused. '*He* said to say he doesn't like you.'

I could hear Mum's thoughts. (*You've gone and done it, Camille, haven't you?*).

Asha bashed her hand on the door, and we all jumped. 'You arsehole.' She punched the door. 'You liar.' She grabbed my arms, she shook me really hard.

'Asha, why don't we go for a walk, take some time out?' The Queen said, desperate to be of help.

'I can't go out for a walk, you fucking idiot,' Asha said.

The Queen did not understand, she did not know what I was dealing with here. Although, come to think of it, she should. She should have known. She was witnessing it. So were Mum and Dad. So was the red-head. It's just like the broken nose, everyone was minimising it, dismissing it.

'These two have been having such a hard time,' Mum said. 'At each other all the time, they're just like my brothers, these two.'

These two? What did any of this have to do with me?

'My sister pushed me through a window once,' the red-head said.

'Asha, Camille,' The Queen said, 'you two need to have some space. You've got your own rooms now, why don't you take time out, like we talked about?'

She moved towards Asha, which made Asha move towards her. No way – was she going to punch The Queen?

'Do not come near me, get the fuck away from me, you dumb old bag.'

Poor The Queen. I'm going to check on her tomorrow.

Asha grabbed a clay sculpting tool from the table – totally the smallest, it was so blunt – and returned to me slowly as everyone watched – doing, saying, nothing to stop her. She barricaded me against the door again, the weapon in her hand. Instead of stabbing me with it, she held it against her own neck with such drama. She had all the power, she was loving it. She took her time to look at each of the shaky people in the hall. She wasn't pressing the sculpting tool hard. Her skin wasn't anywhere near breaking, it was hardly even making an indent. She said she was going to kill herself if anyone came close and if I didn't read her the text message.

'I'm not reading you my message you fucking nutcase,' I said.

Before I knew it she had downed her suicide tool and head butted me. The back of my head bashed against the door. My brain shook.

I think Asha must have surprised herself. When I could see properly again I realised she was not barricading me anymore. This was my moment. I opened the door and ran out.

DD, why didn't I shut the door behind me, why didn't I keep running, why did I stand on the pavement, waiting for Asha to notice that I was SO close, tantalisingly close, holding the phone up and reading the message to myself? (*Hey Cam, so lovely to meet you. We wish it was under different circumstances. Hope you got home safe? Message us any time, better still, come see us. R and R* ☺ *xxx*)

By the time I'd finished reading it, my face was a smiley one too. Asha was staring at me from the doorway, the four adult-adults standing behind her.

'Tell me the message,' she said.

'Why don't you come out and read it yourself?' I suggested. 'Your bracelet won't beep so close to the house, will it? I'm only about five feet away.'

'Camille, for god's sake,' Mum said. 'Stop it. You're embarrassing all of us.'

I took ten large steps back till I was in the middle of the road. It seemed less dangerous than being inside the house.

'Oh hang on, it'll definitely beep here.' I pressed delete. 'Oops, I deleted it,' I said, then turned and headed to town.

Asha screamed at me as I walked: 'You are evil! You are damned! You are going to hell! Mum, Mu-um, stop her. She is the devil. Look what she does to me, can you believe her? Are you seeing this? I'm going to kill her. I'm going to fucking kill you, Camille! I'm going to fucking murder you.'

'Perhaps one of you might consider calling the police,' I yelled. Even if they heard me, it's pretty clear now that no-one did, or ever would. It was sister stuff, sibling rivalry. It was natural, funny even. Everyone laughs about sibling fights. Like Mum's brother, Poor Frankie, who hasn't left his house in twenty years; and like the red-head whose sister nearly sliced her in two with a window pane. Asha is my shared historian, after all. She's going to be my longest relationship.

Asha threw a few things in my direction, but I didn't look back to see what. Too angry to meet my friends, I headed to a posh bar that they'd never be seen dead in. I ordered a pot of tap water – I had no money, I HAVE no money. I assumed some sleaze bag would offer to buy me a real drink. No-one did. I must have looked like shit. I walked home around midnight and jumped over the fence into the back courtyard. The lights were off in the kitchen. I couldn't see anyone, but even from outside I could hear Mum and Dad fighting in the mezzanine. It seemed safe to creep up and slide open the doors. As I tip-toed through the kitchen I could hear Mum and Dad yelling about Vanessa.

The hall was a mess. Clay and broken stuff everywhere. Asha's bedroom light was on and I could hear her praying. Once in my room, also a filth-pit, I pushed the desk up against the door and sat against it.

BEEP! Shit I should have turned my phone off. Asha would defo hear it – I could hear her praying. She didn't stop praying. Maybe she hadn't heard.

It was from the two Rs:

All okay? R and R x

All good, I replied. *Home safe and sound* ☺

જ

There's clay everywhere, a lot of my clothes are ruined, including and especially my yellow jumpsuit. I'm too scared to have a shower. I've decided to go to Spock's in the morning. Spock's a bogan, Asha says, but at least he's not mad as a snake, and anyway Asha can get fucked. I have to get this out first. I am angry. I am livid. I am going as crazy as my sister, who's only marginally madder than my mother.

Asha's swaying and praying in her room. Mum and Dad are still arguing in the mezzanine. I have to write to stay sane. I must not leave this room. I must not ask Asha to shut the fuck up and stop ruining everyone's lives. What's that now? She's chanting about Nellie again, omg:

'Rise, rise, come back to us, come back to us Nellie, we miss you, we need you, we want to watch you dance, we want to hear your giggles.'

And what's that? She's growling like she did when Granddad Moloney died. Is that supposed to be tongues? Ha. I'm recording it now. Hang on. So funny. It's not tongues, it's Robbie Burns. Moving closer – okay, my phone is against the wall. This is what my big sister is saying next door: '…lang mae abidi abidi woo ha brrrr, tela tela tela kithe kithe hai…' That last bit sounds like Punjabi. Now she's back to the growl she uses for grief, and now she's doing a hoo-ha and a woo-ha and a lang mae and a brrr and a sairie sairly sairt lang mae yer lum reek woo ha brrr. Totally Burns. Tongues! It's good to laugh, but I must do it more quietly.

Someone has just thrown something. Mum, probably, throwing things at Dad. Keep writing, Cammy, keep writing.

Shit, I think that Dad just slammed the front door. Gonna check.

It's him, he's taken a suitcase and two bags with some of his old *Herald* newspapers.

Shit, that's Asha knocking on my door. The desk is backed up against it and I will not let her in. Don't let her in. Cammy, do not let her in. Shit shit shit shit, gotta go hide you, gotta go.

❧

Later: I didn't let Asha in. I told her she was scaring me. I said if she broke my door down I'd call the police. She stood at the door for ages. I could hear her breathing really fast.

'Why would I break your door down?'

She was trying so hard to act human.

'I'm just wanting to see if you're okay.' She paused. 'Dad texted to say he's at the Western Inn. Mum's really upset. I've been making endless cups of tea and brushing her hair.'

She waited for me to say something.

'I'm going back to her now, gonna give her a foot massage.'

She has played this card a lot in the last two weeks – who am I kidding, in the last twenty-one years – that she is the one who cares about and understands and helps our mother. Me, on the other hand – I'm the lazy selfish one who spends one hundred per cent of my time indulging in fun or in self-pity.

'Why can't you be nicer to Mum?' she said the other day. 'She's so down and worried and lonely. Dad doesn't seem to care about her at all, and she does everything for him. She does everything for you too, Camille. How long have you been living here for free? Do you ever pay for food? Are you ever going to get a job? She gave birth to you, breast fed you, she gave up her career for you.'

Just for *me?* And which career exactly: modern dance, part-time admin worker, sandwich maker, or did she mean empty-nest influencer?

Anyway, I know Asha doesn't really want me to help Mum. She likes to be the one who's close to her, who's properly loving. What Asha always wants is praise and a favour. I don't want to do her another favour and I have a terrible sick feeling in my tummy – probably because she is trying to behave like a human – that she is going to ask me to do one really soon.

ↄ

Later, god, it's ten past three: Asha and Mum fell asleep on the sofa a little while ago. I've hidden what's left of the wine (you know where, I love that only you and I know where, DD). I'm not gonna make a sound, don't want to wake them. Crazy bitches. Since Dad left they've been taking turns to howl, and now they're spooning, which is especially creepy cos Asha's the outer. I'd join Dad at the Western Inn if he was definitely alone there. For his sake, I hope he's not, I hope the red-headed divorcee from the Eureka Theatre is laughing at his jokes and kissing him kindly and making him feel good about himself, valued, like he should be, because he is utterly gorgeous and always generous and writing about him is making me cry. I could do with a red-headed step-mother, tbh, I could do with any mother other than the one I've got. She is a fuckhead. She is a selfish, lazy fuckhead. She is the same as Asha. They both have the same problem, don't know what it is though. Every time I look up their symptoms a different condition seems to fit: depression, anxiety, alcoholism, bipolar, ADHD, narcissism defo, anger-management issues FOR SURE. The one that keeps popping up is personality disorder, but I don't like thinking it's that one, cos there's no medicine for it, all you can do with those fuckheads is get them out of your life, which is what I am going to do, DD, after what happened today – yesterday now. That is exactly what I am going to do. I've packed my bags, and when it's not stupid o'clock I'm trying Spock's number again and I'm moving in with him, even though he's never asked me to, even though we're not even boyfriend and girlfriend officially yet, even though he lives with his big brother, Big John, and Big John is a total idiot who thinks Scotland is in England.

∽

It's 5am, still too early to turn up at Spock's. I think Asha and Mum are stirring. Hang on … False alarm, all good I think. Hang on … It's just the telly still, they're watching *Meet, Marry, Murder* or *Who the Fuck Did I Marry?*, or one of those true crime shows they're into with never-ending episodes about betrayal causing throat-slits and poisonings and the sawing of women into tiny little pieces. OMG I am actually still shaking with fear. I have my back against my bedroom door because I am terrified she'll bash it down and smash up my things like she's smashed up everything else tonight. I HATE HER. I am SO tempted to tell Mum and Dad about Nellie, but I won't because I promised.

It's nearly 6am, the sun's up and it's going to be hot again. I am already boiling. I could probably go to Spock's, but I smell, and I am not risking going to the bathroom yet. Dad left hours ago. I need him to come home. In between howling with Mum on the sofa and praying in her room, Asha has tried to get me back on side. I will not be conned. She will not get me back on side. For hours I have been fantasising about killing her; strangling her with my bare hands; smashing my fist into her face again and again till it's wet, stabbing her in the stomach with a much bigger clay tool than the one she put against her neck, wriggling it round inside so it scrapes bone and squelches organs. I want to pull her hair till her scalp skin comes off with it. I want to stamp on her mouth with my biker boots until my foot gets stuck in her skull. I want to put sandpaper on the pottery wheel and hold her cheek against it and press the pedal till 'the good side' of her face comes off. I want to drug her unconscious and cover her mouth and nose with wet clay, and watch her legs and arms wriggle till it starts to dry.

Oh boy, I really need a shower.

'Camille?'

Fuckety fuck, that's her again.

'Cammy, are you awake?'

I am not responding. She will not oi me, I will not be oi'd. And I am never, ever, EVER, doing her another favour as long as we both shall live, AMEN.

CHAPTER ELEVEN

The Therapist

Joy didn't spend a cent on Sunday. She'd need several money-free days to get back on budget after the open house with family number nine. Poor things, they needed the dosh more than she did. They also needed a lot more therapy. What a time they were having; unhealthy relationships in every direction. She hardly knew where to start. They seemed to be stuck in perpetual lockdown, one daughter unable to leave, the other stubbornly unwilling. So many families had spiralled into toxicity after the virus, many surfacing with new ideas their loved ones didn't understand. In family number one, for example, the dad and the third-born came out believing the local dry-cleaner's was the centre of a worldwide cabal of Satan-worshiping paedophiles. The two of them never stopped talking about it. Thankfully the thirty-two-year-old third-born left home when lockdown lifted (unvaccinated, as he was all about freedom). But the dad and the mum were still having a terrible time. Last session they fought non-stop because the dad was staking out the sinister shop in the family car every night.

'He's stuffing his gob with doughnuts,' his wife said last session. 'He thinks he's in a movie. And he's so fat I can't even look at him.'

Unhappy families all around. More work for Joy, which gave her a mixture of guilt and gratitude.

But she wasn't going to think about work. Today she would be concentrating on Jeanie, who was coming home tomorrow, after three long months. She would be moving to a new environment, which might be just the thing. She wouldn't be reminded of her dad all the time – the plum tree he planted, the barbecue he built, the height marks he made on the kitchen wall, the Christmas turkeys he carved at the mahogany dining table he polished (and which Joy sold to Mr and Mrs Yung). The unit wasn't so bad really, not once the beds were made up with crisp, fresh sheets and the right lighting sorted. The extortionate scented candles she bought the previous night were helping to mask the odd smell. What was that? And while she could hear what her new neighbours were watching on television – reality, mostly, lots of yelling – they were more friendly than the ones she had in Lake Wendouree. Mr and Mrs Barnard, who had lived at number fourteen, were a pair of mean old snobs. When Joy told them she was moving to Sebastopol, Mrs Barnard actually gasped and said: 'Oh lord, Joy, it's a dump. The druggies all live there.' Joy would never say something like that to anyone, no matter where they lived. Mrs Barnard realised immediately that she had made a faux pas, not about Joy's new suburb, but about Jeanie. She knew fine well – like everyone within a two-kilometre radius of the lake – that Jeanie had grappled with addiction since her father's death.

'We'll fit right in then,' Joy said, hoping never to see Mrs Barnard and her scrawny bald husband and their three ridiculous cars ever again. Joy intended to embrace the diversity of her new area. She would not miss the lake or the garden or the endless, grief-filled walks listening to the same song over and over. She certainly would not miss the pretentious and intolerant residents of her picture-postcard parade.

Already, three of her new neighbours had popped by to welcome her and had given very handy advice about local facilities, alarm systems and refuse collection. One of them, Yolanda, presented her with muffins. Bought ones, but very tasty. Joy didn't need lunch after.

She worked hard all day unpacking and making the place her own. It was going to work this time, she told herself. This time, Jeanie would stay off that terrible Ice and be herself again. She was certain of it. So was Jeanie's key worker at rehab.

'She's never been so motivated,' her key worker said at the pre-discharge meeting. 'Absolutely determined. She has part-time work set up at the florist in Ballan, just ten hours a week, which is a sensible start. She has cut off all ties with her drug-using friends. She's had enough, haven't you Jeanie?'

'I'd rather die than use again,' Jeanie had said. 'And if I use again I will die anyway. I have, Mum, I have had enough. Third time lucky.'

Joy was so excited she couldn't sleep on Sunday night. Her little girl was coming home. Her little girl of forty-three.

૯૭

This was the third time Joy had collected Jeanie from rehab. The first time was just after Bertie's death, but raw grief wasn't why she cried all the way there. Jeanie had only been in the facility for seven days when a staff member caught her buying drugs from another resident. She was kicked out immediately. She no longer had a home to go to and she had no job. Joy had begged her to come back home with her. She would make her soup. They would go on long walks. They would watch movies, play board games, listen to music, bake cakes. Alas, Jeanie asked to be dropped off at her friend's house in the country. His name was Mike and he was no good. There was a sofa in his front garden as well as a lot of car parts, but no actual cars. Apart from insisting on going to Mike's, Jeanie didn't talk for the entire trip. She just sat there, scratching her neck and rocking back and forth. She opened the car door before the engine stopped and didn't even say goodbye, racing into Mike's house to do whatever it was meth users did.

Next time, Jeanie saw out seven weeks of the three-month programme. Joy had paid for it with what little was left of Bertie's pension as well as her own superannuation from the part-time dental nursing she had dipped in and out of till Bertie died. Joy refused to take her to Mike's. When Jeanie asked to go to Nathan's, who Joy didn't know, she also refused. They argued all the way to Lake Wendouree, where her daughter remained for two long and horrid days. Walks and boardgames were sullen and often turned into tantrums. Even baking was sour. Joy was almost glad when her daughter ran away in the middle of the night to Mike's or Nathan's, or someone else's who was no good.

It was understandable that she was sick to the stomach as she made this third and final drive. There was very little money left to try this again, and she was terrified that she might greet a scratching and rocking Jeanie who would ask to be dropped off somewhere with rusty car parts on the grass.

Think positive, Joy said to herself, country music blaring in Bertie's precious BMW. An extravagance, the car. She had often considered selling it and buying a Toyota, especially since Jeanie had repeatedly driven it without permission and like a teenage hoon. It had been impounded three times in the last two years. But it was her only remaining luxury, and it smelt of Bertie. And while Bertie reminded her mostly of disinfectant and poor financial decision-making, the scent calmed her in this situation. She was not the single mother of a 'druggie', she was not alone.

She had no need for nerves. Jeanie had completed the full programme this time. She had made plans. She had emailed every florist in the western district and secured a part-time job, starting tomorrow. She had drawn up a daily and weekly routine: yoga, reading, baking, working, walking. She had dropped her anti-social drug-using friends. Best of all, she wanted – actually, she had pleaded – to live with her mother for a few months 'at least'.

'I know I need the support,' she had said at the pre-discharge meeting. 'I want your help, Mum.'

There was nothing sweeter to Joy's ears than these words. Her daughter needed her, wanted her.

She arrived ten minutes early, and Jeanie was waiting on the veranda with a smile, her suitcase packed. She raced towards the car and gave Joy a huge hug. What a feeling. Joy tried to lift her like she did when Jeanie was a child, but she was a weak old woman now and only managed to tighten the squeeze.

Jeanie sang on the way home. She didn't rock or scratch or even change the music. 'Can you drive by the old house?' she said when they reached Ballarat.

'Are you sure?'

'Yeah, do you mind?'

Joy stopped on the other side of the parade. The new

residents were already ripping the place apart. There was a portaloo in the garden. The rockery had been flattened.

'Bye, house,' Jeanie said.

Joy took her hand, expecting tears. But Jeanie smiled. 'Let's go home.'

༄

Joy hadn't been so happy in years. Her daughter was her old self. She wasn't poor Jeanie, she was positive Jeanie, energetic Jeanie, loving, beautiful, kind Jeanie.

'I love that it's small,' Jeanie said. 'You had too much stuff, Mum. Stuff everywhere. Honestly, Dad's clothes freaked me out. I didn't think you'd ever get rid of them, and I know I wouldn't have been able to do it.'

She marvelled as she explored the house and area: the shops are just round the corner; I can walk to McDonald's; the windows open; check the pressure of this shower; it doesn't go from hot to cold with no warning; the courtyard catches the afternoon sun; the folk next door are lovely; it's cool in here for November; I bet it'll cost next to nothing to heat in winter.

Over tea and sandwiches in the courtyard, they planned flower beds together, and decided to do long daily walks. 'Countryside one day, town the next,' Jeanie said. 'Let's see new things. God, I love that the Barnards aren't eye-balling us from their ugly gazebo. I love it here, Mum, thank you. Thanks for everything.'

Joy was a little nervous leaving Jeanie in the afternoon. She had sessions with families numbers three and five. Poor three, the infidelity had halted but the bowel cancer hadn't. And the remaining members in family number five cried non-stop the entire session. But both wanted to see her again, they were hanging in there, working hard at it, because they believed that blood is thicker than water; that a happy family is an early heaven; that with family no-one gets left behind or forgotten. Joy smiled all the way back to Sebastopol. And all the way through to Wednesday afternoon, during which time she and Jeanie enjoyed a sun-filled falling-in-love style montage:

Mother packs daughter a healthy and imaginative lunch and hands it to her at the front door.
Cut to
Mother blows daughter a kiss as she heads off to work in the BMW.
Cut to
Daughter brings mother beautifully arranged begonias home from work.
Cut to
Mother and daughter eat McMuffins on the walk back from the local shops.

Cut to

Mother and daughter listen to the same song as they zig-zag (some of) Mount Buninyong.

Cut to

Mother and daughter bake fairy cakes, eat fairy cakes, play Scrabble.

Cut to

Mother puts on The Crown.

Cut to

Mother makes daughter toast with real salted butter and even dabs of vegemite.

Cut to

Mother fills daughter's bunny mug with hot milk and too many spoons of chocolate.

Cut to

Daughter falls asleep in front of The Crown.

Joy was so happily occupied that she didn't even think to check her phone till Wednesday morning, just after waving Jeanie off the second time.

Rosie had left seven messages:

Sunday: *Hey!! Good luck with the move. Cannot wait to see the new pad. On your phone just press video instead of photo, show me around. Mwah*

Monday: *Hello! How'd it go? Jeanie okay? Click the attachment and check out the restaurant I've booked for our first night.*

It's a short walk from our cottage. Let's get diabetes together! Two weeks to go! Fourteen days! Send me photos if the vid thing is too hard for your feeble, aged brain, Love you so much. Mwah

Monday: *All okay? Tell me you'll get the ticket no matter what. Love you x*

Monday: *Hmm…*

Tuesday: *?*

Tuesday: *Seriously, Joy, pick up. I'm worried. Is she back on it? If you can't buy the ticket I will.*

Tuesday: *Okay, I'm guessing you've got a lot going on. But please, please look after you and not just her. Call me when you can x*

Joy had completely forgotten to book her flight to London. That wasn't quite true. She had remembered several times since Monday morning, when she had promised her sister to do it. Every time she drove past Nina Nguyen's a terrible nausea came over her and she found herself pressing on the accelerator. It seemed wrong to book a holiday so soon after Jeanie's rehab, dangerous even. And everything was going so well. Since Jeanie came home she had experienced something resembling euphoria, a feeling she had not experienced for several decades or more. She didn't want to leave her little girl. Not yet. But she would. Soon.

After deleting several attempts at a message to her sister, Joy decided she would get it right – and press send – after her 3pm therapy session, which was with family number nine.

It was 2pm. Jeanie's shift finished at 1pm. She said she'd be home at 1.30 and that she'd bring pies from the lovely bakery near her work before Joy drove to the Moloney-Singhs. She wished Jeanie had a mobile, but part of her sobriety plan was to be phoneless.

'Too easy to dial those bad numbers,' Jeanie had said at the pre-discharge meeting. 'Far too tempting. I'll go dinosaur and stick to the landline so you can keep an eye.'

Joy almost rang the florist in Ballan but decided not to. Jeanie was probably still working away. It might be a good thing, in fact, that she was late. Her new employer might have some big orders and need her for longer; they might be overwhelmed by Jeanie's knowledge, talent, experience and commitment and have asked her to work longer hours. And if she wasn't at work, it would look very bad, her mother calling to check on her. Jeanie's new boss was aware of her stint in rehab and would assume she'd relapsed. Phoning might lose her the job.

By 2.15pm Joy had no choice but to drive the van to town. Before heading off she texted the second-born:

Hi, Camille, I might be running a few minutes late. Sincere apologies, please hang on for me. See you soon, Mrs S.

CHAPTER TWELVE

The Mum

It couldn't be over. It could not be over. Andeep was hers. She was his. They were supposed to be frolicking in the countryside and making art with all the new mates they were supposed to have made. This was not in the plan. The plan was to fall in love again, to have wild sex again, to be boss-free and child-free and creative, and do whatever the fuck they wanted again. Penny could not get her head around it at all. It simply could not be over. Life without Andeep? She couldn't bear it. She'd been crying since Saturday night. The family therapist was going to arrive any moment, and her husband was still AWOL. Actually, he was still at the Western Inn. Probably with *Vanessa*.

Asha dragged her from sofa to bed on Sunday morning, and she hadn't moved except to wipe the snot and the tears that had poured since he left, and to message him, which she had done dozens of times. No response, nothing. Asha had tried almost as often. Thank god for Asha, who cared.

Camille hadn't even replied when Penny called for her. She hadn't even answered her phone. That girl could spend days alone in her room, doing nothing, ignoring everyone.

She was in Penny's studio room, actually – the private space she needed to get back on track. She was unkind, Camille. Penny didn't expect gratitude or repayment for the years she spent mothering her as a child, but what about all the time and money and love she'd given her as an adult: the extra shifts she worked to pay for her student digs, for example and the last six months here?

'You need to get out of bed now, Mum.' It was Asha. She'd been checking on her by the hour, the blossom. 'She'll be here any minute. I've messaged Dad again. I think he'll come.'

Penny typed a text and copied it to Andeep's Facebook and email:

Are you coming? Please answer. Please come, for the girls.

She didn't mean the thing about the girls, but she knew it would work better than the truth. Please come home for ME. She hadn't eaten in three days, that's how much she missed him. Even if almost everything he did annoyed her. Even if he wasn't funny. Even if she needed alcohol to get through the long days with him. It could not be over because he was hers and not the red-head's with the polka-dot dress.

Penny couldn't stop ruminating about the life drawing that woman had bought, wondering how she could have had the audacity to go up into their mezzanine bedroom like that – and then to come back down the stairs with the painting in her hand and say with nonchalance: 'How much for this?' without a hint of embarrassment. She had held it in such a way that her middle finger was pointing at Andeep's penis, which Penny had not shied away from depicting in all its flaccid, fore-skinned non-glory. Andeep was helping Mrs Salisbury on the pottery wheel at the time. Penny wondered what he'd have said if he witnessed the exchange. Perhaps he'd have confessed right then and there. Although Penny still didn't know if there was anything to confess. Although there must be. Why else would the red-head have held her finger in place the whole time? Why else would she have examined the painting in front of Penny with such trollopy arrogance and say: 'This is really special, it's beautiful. You're very talented. Would one hundred dollars be offensive?' Thinking back, Penny was sure she had a smirk on her freckled, chubby face. She was definitely smirking. And she asked Penny to wrap it in the kitchen before popping it in her bag. She was probably intending to show Andeep at their next 'meeting'. Your wife is clueless, she would probably say. What was she thinking selling it to me? She must know that no-one would buy this other than your best friend, your lover for life, your future wife. The more Penny thought about it, and she thought about it on repeat, the smirking home-wrecker was quite obviously telling her outright. But Penny was not listening because Andeep was hers. Also, her family really needed the one hundred dollars. At that point in the evening they had only sold a couple of candles to Mrs Salisbury.

The doorbell rang and Penny bounced from the bed. It was the first energetic movement she'd made in three days. She stank. She looked terrible. She washed her face in the en-suite, gave her hair a brush, put on her nicest kaftan, then took it off again. If Andeep was still to be hers, she would need to try harder than a tent. She searched for something akin to a polka-dot dress, but all she had was yoga wear, leggings, tents and tunics. In desperation, she opened a zip bag with some precious old dresses she intended to give to the kids. 'Asha, Asha, can you come up?'

Asha came up immediately and whispered, 'Shh, they can hear us. You okay? The therapist is down in the kitchen with Camille.'

'I need to look better than this. What can I wear?'

Asha rummaged through her wardrobe, dismissing items one by one, then turned to the zip bag. 'When all this is over,' she said, 'I am going to take you shopping. For now, wear this.'

She was holding up a tight-fitting halter-neck dress. Penny last wore it to a comedy event in Adelaide, must be almost twenty years ago. She was thirty-four and she was gorgeous. 'I haven't been able to get into that for years.'

'It'll fit now. How long since you've eaten? Your collar bones are sticking right out.'

'Oh, no.'

'Not 'oh no', it's a good thing. Every woman wants jutting clavicles. You look great.'

'You think?'

'I *know*. These shoes.' Asha placed a pair of ankle boots at her feet.

Penny squeezed into the halter-neck, just. 'Isn't it a tad dressy for family therapy?'

'Not in this situation it's not. And the boots dress it down. There, check yourself out.' She twirled her mum towards the mirror. 'You're a skinny bitch.'

'Very,' Penny sobbed.

Asha sorted her hair into a loose bun and messaged her father again. Halfway down the stairs, her phone beeped.

Penny turned around and mouthed, 'Is it him?'

'Yep, he's coming, Mum. I told you he would. He won't leave you, he would never leave us.'

Penny walked down the remainder of the stairs with model confidence. She was thirty-four and irresistible again. Andeep would tell her she was the most beautiful woman in Ballarat, no, in Victoria, Australia, the world. When was the last time he'd said something like that? Only a year or so. She had enjoyed sweet nothings constantly and had stopped appreciating them. They should never have moved from Preston. They were happy there. Idiot Penny; wanting to be happier than that. She took a deep breath and conjured

Preston Penny, Adelaide Penny, most beautiful woman in the world Penny. It was time for family therapy session number two; time to get her husband back.

ဆ

He was wearing new jeans. That was the first thing Penny noticed when Andeep came in, which was a long five minutes after she sat at the table. They were expensive-looking ones that were stupidly skinny; made for young men, or middle-aged ones who are cheating on their wives with red-heads in polka-dot dresses. They couldn't afford jeans like that. What a slap in her face to be spending money at a time like this. He knew there were seven reminders upstairs, including electricity, which they needed far more than a pair of ridiculous jeans.

'Hello,' she said, as if she'd never met him before.

'Hello,' he said, as if he hated her.

He only ever wore 501s. It was a rule. Up there with only ever wearing white T-shirts. He was wearing a blue shirt. With a French tuck. He did not know about such tucks. Someone had Frenched it for him.

Penny shouldn't stare. She should be nonchalant and brazen, like the lover who had obviously taken him shopping. Andeep never went shopping. He would start sighing at the very mention of it. He wouldn't even buy clothes online. In the early years he was dressed by his mother and sisters, who took him to the New Year sales in Glasgow. They knew what he liked (501s, white T-shirts, leather jackets) and were not afraid of his sighs. In recent (impoverished) years, their annual trips to Scotland no longer possible, Penny and the girls bought him his uniform replacements from charity shops, or from outlets, mainly for his birthday and for Christmas. He did not care about clothes. He was not vain.

He looked different in the new jeans. Mean. Hunky. And un-gettable.

She, on the other hand, looked uncomfortable and elderly. She wished she hadn't let Asha dress her. Asha's dress sense had always been dodgy. Penny wasn't used to tight clothing. It was making her anxious and fidgety and sweaty. What was she thinking, going braless? And if her clavicle was jutting then her neck and face bones probably were too. There was probably wrinkly old neck skin flapping about all over the place. She should not move. She should keep her head high. She should thrust her breasts forward. But she was braless so that was not possible.

He was probably avoiding eye contact because the sight of her made him sick. She knew, everyone knew, that a woman her age needed weight to flesh out the wrinkles. Penny was very hot and a little dizzy. Sweat was gathering in her groin area. Or was that urine? Oh god, if she stood up would the seat be wet, would the bum of her tight, green halter-neck have a wet patch on it? Oh god.

The therapist had talked non-stop since they all took their seats. Something about Saturday being stressful and how were they all blah blah. Something about the tasks – yes, they'd moved rooms. Yes, they had all given each other some space. Andeep had, particularly, Penny thought, he's moved the fuck out, he's left me, he's left us (she did not say this out loud) and has spent all our money on jeans. But no, they had not brought three photos with them.

Asha had, actually, but she was the only one. This knocked Mrs Salisbury out of whack. 'Okay,' she said, 'well, we won't do that today then, that's no problem. I would like to know why, though? Camille, why didn't you choose three family photos?'

'I did, but Asha ripped them up,' Camille said.

'And you?' she asked Andeep.

'I did but I forgot to bring my phone,' he said.

'Penny?'

'I did but I've been crying in bed. I'm very, very, down. I'm afraid I forgot, but they were lovely photographs, we chose them together in Hall's Gap, Andeep and I, such beautiful happy family pictures. The first one was—'

The therapist didn't give her a chance to describe the photos, which would have helped with her mission. Andeep would have remembered the precious moments they'd had in Hall's Gap less than one week ago, and the beautiful times they'd had for years and years. Stupid therapist, one of the worst she'd ever experienced. Rude even. Unprofessional, interrupting her like that. And what kind of therapist comes to a client's party? She was blah-blahing to the girls about the photo-ripping incident. Penny would need to find a better therapist.

Andeep had trimmed his beard. Very neat and glossy, a very good job. Penny usually trimmed his beard because he didn't give a shit how he looked and refused to go to the barber's and was useless at doing it himself. He seemed determined not to look at her, no matter how long she looked at him.

The therapist had moved on to talk about the different families children are born into. 'You see this unit in one way,' she said. 'Each sibling thinks they're born into the same family, but actually, every child is born into a completely different situation. Asha,' she said, 'you were born an only child. And the circumstances for your parents were completely different to that of your little sister.'

That's true, Penny thought. When Asha was born they both had jobs. Penny was still managing to laugh at his tiny repertoire of jokes. She was the most beautiful woman in Preston. They were in love.

When Camille was born, they were struggling financially. Andeep was still clinging to his comedy career as well as grieving one of his many 'very close' relatives (sigh). Penny had post-natal depression for a good twelve months, couldn't get out of bed, like she hadn't been able to get out of bed for the last three days. And, of course, they had boisterous three-year-old Asha, who was very jealous of the new baby. One day, Penny found her hovering over the cot holding the pink teddy over Camille's little face. (They were both given teddies. Asha was not pleased about getting the brown one.) That was the only time she smacked Asha. She still felt bad about it.

He was wearing new socks. His eyebrows seemed neater. He smelled funny. Was that a new aftershave? She managed to catch his eye – hoorah. He smiled at her, but it wasn't his usual smile. It was new and sinister. A guilty smile. It was impossible to come to any conclusion other than this: Andeep was definitely fucking Vanessa. Had been for three days solid. If she inhaled slowly through her nose for a long time she could smell it. It wasn't a funny smell, it was fanny. He smelt of fanny. Probably why his beard was so glossy.

She tried to do the breathing someone-or-other had told her to do, but it didn't work. She closed her eyes and imagined inhaling smack, but that made her nauseous. She conjured the black colour instead of the blue colour and panicked. She was so dizzy. She must surely be quite ill. If Andeep looked at her long enough he would notice. She might faint. Not might, would. She would faint, and she did.

‿〜

She woke to his beautiful wee face. She was on the sofa in the living area and he was holding her hand. 'Where is everyone?' she said.

'Scattered.'

His accent was glorious. How she loved his voice.

'How are you feeling? Can you sit up?'

He helped her upright, and her dress ripped. She wasn't sure where. She didn't care. She might have peed when she fainted, or even before, but she didn't care about that either. She could put a kaftan on again and be comfortable because Andeep was here. He held a glass of cold water to her mouth. He cut her a slice of apple, smiled as she ate it. Andeep, water, sugar: all she needed. 'Thank you, honey,' she said, before noticing that he was not taking hold of her hand again and that he wasn't smiling anymore and was moving further away from her, just a few inches but enough for her to know.

'I'm just going to get this all out,' he said.

Fake a smile, Penny, it might well turn into a real one. But that tone, that expression, that beard, those idiot jeans. How dare he, the talentless prick and his wrinkly dick.

'Before Saturday I was having an emotional affair with Vanessa. For a few months. Since the open house it's been physical. I'm not in love with her but I'm not in love with you either.'

Pretend you're inhaling smack, Penny, like the counsellor with the burgundy hair said.

'I don't want to be with you anymore. There's love here still, but it's not good love, it's history, it's parenting-based.'

Invite the blue colour in, Penny, like the mindfulness coach with the gammy leg said.

'Much sadder than that – I don't like you anymore.'

No negative words, Penny, like the posh therapist with the thin lips said.

Penny was drenched. The sofa had a wet patch on it. Her dress had ripped right across her stomach, the squidge was flopping out.

Vanessa. No, no, no, he was hers and she was his. Vanessa?

'I've packed my things. I've hired a lawyer. I don't want any contact. I want a divorce. Goodbye, Penny.'

CHAPTER THIRTEEN

The Second-Born

Sorry I haven't written for so long. I left you at home, only managed to get you back today. I have missed you, DD. So much has happened since that shit-show of an open house. My family is so embarrassing. I am still mortified. And really, really sore.

I didn't fall asleep till after 6am. I wish I'd made it out to Spock's in time. Stupid me, I flaked out on the floor and woke around midday on Sunday with a desk being pushed into me.

'Camille, Cam?'

Asha was trying to get in. I scraped the desk back against the door and pushed it with my hands. She must have been pushing hard too, because my arms started shaking and my veins got huge.

'Are you okay? Why won't you let me in?'

I didn't answer. I had decided never to talk to her again unless words came out while maiming or killing her. I wished I could push the desk hard enough to break the door down and flatten her almost perfectly symmetrical face until it was a centimetre thin and matter oozed out. I wasn't strong enough.

'Just to say I've put Mum to bed. She's in a state. Have you heard from Dad?'

Don't say a word, Cam, not a word, I told myself. She always used Dad to get me back on side. Or Mum. Or sisterhood, whatever that is. She's always thought she's entitled to me; that she deserves undying loyalty from me. While living together in that horrible house she had a growing list of reasons why I owed her, eg:

'We are sisters. I am your big sister. I am a good sister.'

(Two out of three ain't bad, but so what, what does that mean anyway?)

'I taught you how to play netball.'

(I have always hated it, oh and you broke my nose 'playing netball' you mental case.)

'I showed you how to do your hair like that.'

(I hate it.)

'You'd dress like a dag if not for me.'

(You are the daggiest dresser in Ballarat, and that is saying something.)

'I always talk you through it when you get upset.'

(You're always the reason I get upset.)

It goes on and on. And on. So does her list about the ways in which I have disappointed her over the years, for example:

'You never call me.'

(Because I hate talking to you.)

'You don't look after things, you don't show any respect

for my belongings, you stained my favourite shirt that time and never fixed it.'

(It was 2009.)

'You put no thought into birthday presents.'

(I don't want to give you birthday presents, I don't want birthday presents from you, no matter how perfect and thoughtful they are. I know I will react poorly to them, under-appreciate them. I may not even understand them. Thinking about presents is making me sore. Itchy. Oh god. I need a pillow. I need a different top. Your presents and your birthdays scare the shit out of me.)

'You don't thank me for all the work I do around the house.'

(I would rather live in a pool of diarrhoea than deal with your rage when you clean, you lunatic.)

'Open the door, Camille,' she said, 'you're worrying me, do you want me to kick it in?'

I tightened my push against the desk. She may have heard my breathing. I hope so. I could hear hers.

She calmed it down to re-humanise: 'Okay, no worries, I'm just finishing cleaning up. Omg what a mess.'

Yes, I thought, because you smashed everything up.

'Just to say we have no food at all. Dad won't answer his phone, can you believe him? What an arsehole.'

Here we go – whose side am I on? If I didn't pick the right one, I would get it. Dad's, I was on Dad's.

(Wrong.)

'Can you try him, maybe? Mum can't even move. And obviously I can't go out. I'll go to jail if I go out – you do understand that, don't you? Could you please go to the shops for me and Mum and get bread and milk and stuff and something for dinner...'

Wait for it, wait for it...

'...and wine? I thought we had at least two goon sacks left. I can't find them anywhere. Have you got them in there? Where did you put them? Camille? Camille!'

We had two goon sacks and six bottles, to be exact. In my secret hiding place.

She gave up and started cleaning again, huffing and puffing and swearing as she vacuumed – which is how Asha and Mum clean – not with grace, but with fury. I could hear everything she was saying, even when she was out the back:

'What the fuck is that doing there?

'Who left this in the sink, has no-one heard of rinsing?

'Bunch of grotty arseholes. Pigs. This is a pigsty.

'Just plain rude leaving this on the loo for me to scrape off with this disgusting brush. Why isn't there bleach in the container? Gross.' She faked a dry heave.

'Why would anyone leave a tube of toothpaste in this state? Camille, WHY? What is wrong with you? All you have to do is squeeze it, from the bottom up, and roll it, and ROLL IT so the next person can get some out. It's manners, it's common sense.'

I put my earphones in and turned the volume to maximum. I waited for an hour, but it wasn't safe to leave, she was still banging about and swearing, waiting for me to react and/or come out.

Eventually I had to pee in a jug that hadn't hardened yet. Most of it was absorbed into the wet clay but quite a lot dribbled onto the stone floor. God, it is the most uncomfortable house. Stone floors, who wants stone floors in a bedroom, or in any room? Not Dad, he wanted carpet, like me. How Mum and Asha scoffed – 'Cover these floors? They're *listed,* they're bluestone.' After an hour I made a mistake. I lay on the gym mat and closed my eyes and listened to heavy metal, which was calmer than listening to my sister.

A while later, I could hear scraping. I could feel someone touching my hand. It was nice at first. No-one had held my hand in a long time, not even Spock. He's always too wasted and too manly to hold hands. Something was banging into my leg. Weird, what's that? I thought, then I woke up.

Asha was standing over me. She'd pushed the door and moved the desk to get in while I was sleeping to AC/DC, hence the scraping. The hand hold was her pressing my fingerprint against my phone, like last time. She was now in possession of my mobile, standing what seemed about a mile above me, and kicking my leg.

'Oi, wake up, oi.'

Another kick, ouch. Earphones off, I tried to sit up, but she put her foot on my stomach and pushed me back down. She kept her foot there and pressed, immobilising me.

'Hey, I can't breathe,' I tried to say.

She didn't care. She was looking at my phone. 'I knew it,' she said.

'Ow, Asha stop, Asha, Asha, I can't breathe.'

She released her foot a bit, angry eyes on my phone.

I pounced to my feet and lunged at her. 'Give it back.'

She held it to the side, her other arm fending me off with slaps, and read a message: 'Saturday night. From an unknown number.'

Oops, I had deleted the first text from Rowena as well as her number from my contacts list. But I had failed to block her number entirely and delete the second message.

'*All ok?*' Asha read. '*R and R, kiss.*'

She placed great emphasis on the kiss.

'And this is what you replied to Richard and Rowena, who you say you didn't speak to in Geelong at all: "All good. Home safe and sound, *smiley face.*" You saw them, I knew it, you were with them all day, you liar, what did they say, what were you doing? Tell me or I'll punch you in the face.'

'Do it,' I said, moving closer. 'Why not? You've already broken my nose and head-butted me.'

'I broke your nose? What rubbish. Why didn't you ring

an ambulance, then? You're just mad because you can't catch. I did not break your nose, you whiney, dobbing wimp.'

(She was getting very good at rewriting history.)

'You're such a liar. I can't believe you've betrayed me like this…'

(This will undoubtedly be added to list B above.)

'…your own sister, your only sister. After everything I have done for you.'

(See list A.)

'You're evil, Camille, you are pure evil. Step away from me or I'll do it. I will smash your face in with my fist.'

She was shaking her knuckles two inches from my chin – they were as tight and as white as her lips.

'You just kicked me, Asha, you just stepped on my stomach. A punch in the face doesn't scare me. Go on, go on.' I stood tall, chin out, daring her. 'Do it.'

She punched me in the face.

Fuck. If I hadn't been prepared for it, feet slightly apart, strong and stiff as a board, I would have toppled. I was too angry for it to hurt. Slowly I turned my head, offering her the other side. Understanding the reference, she refrained from punching it.

'Give me the phone,' I said, but she was holding it behind her back now, refusing. In my attempt to retrieve it I may have shoved her a little. She didn't fall over. She didn't even bash her back against the wall. It made her even angrier, though, and she hurled herself at me with an animal growl. She pressed the phone against my throat. I couldn't breathe.

'What were you doing in Geelong, what were they saying? Why are you torturing me, why are you lying to me?'

Fuck her, I wasn't going to tell her anything, ever, no matter how close I was to death.

She pushed me, and I fell to the ground, banging my back into the pottery wheel. Still on the floor, I defended myself by twirling the wheel and pointing my elbows as she jabbed at me with the edge of the phone. Phones are hard, DD, they hurt if you hold them the right way. I started crawling towards the door, over the toppled desk. She bashed my back with the phone with each movement. When I got to the door, she hit me so hard in the back of the neck that I was flattened on the stone. I stayed still for a few seconds, played dead. This made her stop and worry, I think, which was enough time for me to get to my feet. I reached for the door. She hit my neck again. She was going to seriously injure me. If she could, she would kill me. No way, I thought, no fucking way is she going to kill me. I turned and pushed her and she fell back onto the gym mat.

'Ow, ow, my arm, you crazy bitch.' She pretended to be hurt, she started whimpering. She'd fallen on faux sheepskin ffs.

I seized the moment – and the phone – and ran out into

the hall. I yelled for Mum, but she didn't hear, or didn't care enough to answer, then I raced out the door and didn't stop running till I got to Spock's.

∽

His mate Barnsey came to the door, so off his head on Ket that he couldn't get any words out, despite trying really hard for a really long time. I could see Spock and his big brother, Big John, sprawled on the floor in the lounge and thought twice about going in. It probably wouldn't be worse than home, but it was a close call. Spock was getting druggier every time I saw him.

'Get on in.' Spock had managed to sit up. 'It's my darlin', it's my little Campervan.'

He called me something different every time I saw him, prided himself on it. Last time it was either Camisole or Camera-obscura, can't remember which. He couldn't get all the way up to give me a kiss. I patted his head.

'What the fuck's happened to you?' said Big John.

I realised I was limping and probably had bruises. 'Bar brawl,' I said. 'Mind if I hang for a bit?'

Barnsey tried to say something, it made all of us laugh.

'You look like you could do with some non-reality,' Spock said, offering me a plate filled with pills and powder and crystals.

'What kind of mate pushes that stuff?' I said to Spock, who was popping crystals in a glass pipe.

'We're not mates,' he said, lighting up.

'Are we not?'

'We're lovers.'

Barney tried to say something – think it was 'lovers'. We all waited for him to give up then laughed again.

Big John took the glass pipe and had a smoke.

I hated hanging round people on meth. Last time, Spock danced for ten hours then wrote a very short fantasy novel in a language he didn't understand then crashed his car into his dad's office. Another time Archie from Sovereign Hill had a psychotic episode and started plucking the hairs on his legs till he somehow made himself bleed. Said there were spiders inside his hands and that the devil was real and was standing right behind me.

'Judgey judgey,' said Big John, taking another puff. 'What kind of mate wouldn't want to share euphoria?' He bounced up from the floor, grabbed a guitar and started playing something beautiful and classical. Who'd have known.

Some non-reality was exactly what I needed and I was pretty close, I reckon, to partaking. Apart from Barnsey they all looked really happy. Imagine being happy. Y'know, DD, I don't think I can imagine. It's been so long. What even is it?

'Have you got coffee?' I headed to the grotty kitchen of

this shared bachelor pad/drug den. To my surprise, they even had fresh milk.

'You all right, Cameltoe?' Spock was in the kitchen now, wanting a hug.

'Do you and Big John ever fall out?' I asked.

'Argue?'

'Yeah, like physically as well.'

'Not really,' he said. 'He's a fucking giant.'

'He's never hurt you?'

'Nah … Hey BJ,' he yelled to his brother next door, 'have you ever hurt me?'

'Nah,' Big John yelled from the lounge.

Spock nodded, happy they agreed, then remembered something and yelled again: 'What about that time you opened the car door in Napier Street and pushed me out?'

'Oh yeah, haha.'

'Hahaha,' Spock laughed. 'Mum and Dad grounded his fat arse.'

'For six months!' Big John added.

'Asha driving you nuts, eh?' Spock said.

'A bit.' I melted into his arms again, they're the only things about him that I like tbh.

'Tell you what, take this as an introductory gift from me.' He handed me a small tin. 'I think what you need is…'

'Euphoria!' That came from Barnsey next door. He was very pleased to get it out so quickly.

Big John applauded him.

'So you really are dealing this shit now?'

'Only to mates.'

'We're not mates, remember?' I said, foregoing the coffee, disengaging from his arms and heading out the back door as fast as I could.

With the tin, DD. Dunno why, hate to admit it, but I took the tin.

&

Dad's phone was going straight to voicemail. The receptionist at the Western Inn sounded like she knew him intimately and said with affection that he was at the Eureka, rehearsing. I had no idea what he was rehearsing for but I assumed Vanessa would be there too so I didn't bother going. Actually, fuck him, leaving like that. Fuck him, fuck Mum and fuck Asha.

I had no money to get to Melbourne. Without thinking, I phoned Rowena. It took her ages to answer and I nearly chickened out.

'Hello,' she said.

'Rowena, it's Camille,' I said.

A pause, then she said: 'I thought I told you never to call me.' Her voice low and sinister.

'Did you?' I asked.

'If you ever call me or my husband again, we will phone the police,' she said, and hung up.

Omg, psycho! I was totally head-fucked. Poor Asha. She's been head-fucked by these two as well. I was really angry, really upset. In desperation I texted The Queen:

Hey Mrs Salisbury, just wondering if you know where homeless people go?'

What do you mean? she replied.

I can't live at Mum and Dad's anymore. I've left. I have absolutely no money. I just need somewhere to stay for a while, probs till Friday when Asha goes to court. She'll go back to Sunshine after that. Is there a homeless hostel in Ballarat?

Do you drive? she typed.

I do. (Mind you, I hadn't for a long time.)

I have a van. You can have that till Friday if you want.

Really? I was tearful. *That would be incredible.*

Where are you? I'll come get you.

❧

Ah this van, I love it. I never want to leave. Since Sunday I've been driving round the western district, eating baked beans and the other stuff Mrs Salisbury gave me, and sleeping soundly in lay-bys. There's a huge dental chair in the middle that I'm sitting on now, which is crazy comfy. Not sure I'll ever tire of zuzzing it up and down. Makes me giggle every time. There's a tiny kitchenette for cooking and a cupboard with all sorts of sharp dental implements that I could slice people with if they tried to break in at night. Proper torture cupboard, it is, with syringes, pickers and drills. Asha has messaged me hundreds of times, and it's entertaining reading – she goes from aggro to entitled to fake loving to livid to indignant and back to fake loving again. She is so desperate to know what happened in Geelong, that is all she cares about. She wants to know if I'm still in contact with the Rs. She wants Richard to know she is praying, that she hasn't given up. (I know what she means. Praying for Nellie. Nutter!) She wants to see Richard. She loves him. Do I not understand? He loves her too, she knows he does, was it obvious to me when I spoke to him, that he loves her too? It's his wife, she's manipulating him, she's just doing damage control because she wants to keep him, she likes being the pastor's wife, she likes the money, don't I reckon, don't I think?

Ugh, she makes me sick to the stomach. I never want to see her again. I might block her number. Ooh, why haven't I done that? I am going to block her number.

BLOCKED! Ha. Oh, I just breathed out for so long. What a relief. I don't need to have any contact with her ever again. Ever again.

I've had plenty of time on my hands out here. When the signal is good I've done some digging about the affair 'scandal'. I hate to agree with Asha about anything but it does seem like a cover up.

'Pastor in Love Triangle.'

'Pastor Unfaithful to Grieving Wife.'

'Pastor Dumps Lover.'

'Pastor Assaulted by Crazed Mistress at Prayer Meeting.'

'I Love My Wife, Pastor Says, Crying.'

Whoopitydooda. Hardly a big deal compared to the shit churches usually get involved in. Child abuse, obvs, and grave-soaking. There are folk all over the place lying on graves to suck the holy ghost out of the dead. I dug deep enough to find stuff about waking up Nellie too. It's not just Asha. And here's the big news – the two Rs started it. They raised money to raise Nellie. They laid her out as long as they were allowed and chanted around her body, saying the same things Asha was saying in her room – wake up, Nellie, we want to see your smiling face, we want to hear your beautiful voice, etc etc. They wrote and sold songs, and held meetings. Lots and lots of people believed the power of prayer could bring her back. It's actually not so mad if you buy into Christianity. If you believe Jesus healed, if you believe he brought Lazarus back, then why not? Like Matthew says: 'Heal the sick, cleanse the lepers, raise the dead, cast out demons.'

Dance Said He denounced the whole thing ages ago. So did the two Rs (in public). But there are still people out there like Asha praying for Nellie's resurrection, even though she's six feet under in Meredith. And there are dead-raising teams all over Facebook – DRTs! They're as common as local buy-and-sell groups. All you gotta do is believe. All you gotta do is pray really hard and send in money. When I think back to what Rowena said in Geelong – 'Tell her we're glad she's praying, tell her not to stop believing. She shouldn't give up.' I realise they are still doing it, The Dick and Rowena. They're wrapping presents for her birthday ffs. They're waiting for her to finish her jigsaw puzzle. It's kind of comforting to know Asha's madness is not unique to her, that she wasn't always bat-shit crazy, just moderately so; that she's been brainwashed. I still hate her though, I'm not going to feel sorry for her.

It's Wednesday evening now. I went home for family therapy because I promised Dad I would. I didn't talk to Asha the whole time, even with her staring me out (wondering how best to get through to me: angry stare, scary stare, fake kind stare, killer stare, sisterhood stare). It was safe with Mrs S there. I think she might be the kindest person in the universe. I wish she was my mum. The session was useless though. No-one noticed me limping on the way in, or the bruises on my face and arms, or the marks on my neck. I didn't bother telling them what Asha did to me on Sunday. Mum fainted before anyone got to say anything meaningful, anyhow. Then Dad left Mum for good.

Seriously, fuck Dad. Our family is four fucked people fucking each other over. It is over. I am over it.

I'm sore still. My chin aches and I have bruises everywhere, all over my back and arms and elbows. I can't turn my head without wincing. I probably should have gone to A&E. I probably should have told the doctors and the nurses what Asha did. But I know what they'd say: *Siblings*! And they'd laugh about the time their sister broke their arm or the time they threw a vase at their brother and he had to get stitches, hahaha, or something like that.

I'm in the loveliest spot, beach this time, looking out over the majestic limestone stacks on the shore – The Twelve Apostles – and they really are wow, they make me gooey, like I've been thinking too small, too inside myself, and that I should look up and out more. I might stay right here till Friday. There's tons of beans and soup and noodles and chocolate and crackers in the cupboard. God bless Mrs Salisbury. In fact, I think I'll text her same:

Heating soup on the fabby wee stove: God bless you Mrs S xxx

CHAPTER FOURTEEN

The Therapist

By Wednesday night Joy's savings – and therefore the number of years she could afford to be alive – had dwindled again. Only by six days – three hundred dollars – but it scared her, thinking of lost days. She could imagine what to do with days. She would not be gloomy about it. She still had enough money to make it to eighty-four if she stuck to the budget. She sighed at the thought of eighty-four. No-one she knew had any fun in their early eighties (Mrs Valencia Senior from Mount Clear cried from eighty on, every minute of the day; and Rosie's mother-in-law kept getting the train to her childhood neighbourhood around then. She could never find her way back to the care home). Eighty-four would almost certainly be miserable. She'd probably need a zimmer like Mr Benson from the parade and he was only eighty-one. She decided to have a counter meal, why not? It had been a terrible afternoon and evening, and she was starving. She ordered steak Diane and chose a table overlooking the wide road, cars whizzing by as she sipped a lemonade and blackcurrant. So far none of the cars was her BMW.

'Busy day?' the waiter said, delivering her steak.

'Yes, it was,' Joy said. 'Very, as a matter of fact, quite stressful. Thanks so much' – she looked at his badge – 'Gregory. I'm Joy.'

'That's good,' Gregory said, too distracted to continue the conversation.

She really had been busy. What a mess, that family number nine. So much work to do, but at least they all turned up to the second session; at least they were on board to do it. She hated to admit it, but Joy was relieved when the mum fainted. She could end the session and go home. Her tummy was heavy with dread. Please, Jeanie, be home, she thought. Please be home. She drove the van with her head held low, then scolded herself for it. Who cared if her old friends saw her? What did it matter if they assumed she no longer had a BMW? It was becoming very clear that they were old friends already. Not one of them had phoned her or sent her a new-home card. Anne Maclean from the historical society was obviously ignoring her emails. Frank Peters too. And why hadn't anyone phoned her about the begonia festival? She was always involved in the planning meetings this time of the year. Joy had only moved two miles but it seemed she'd moved ten thousand. As for the Barnards and the other residents of her old parade, she wasn't surprised to have had no cards or flowers or visits – she was relieved if anything. She had moved from the most expensive street in Ballarat to the cheapest. She couldn't even afford this counter meal. (The steak was proving rather tough.) And she had a druggie daughter who took her bank card without asking and withdrew three hundred dollars before disappearing. She would not be morose. She would not jump to conclusions. After dinner, she would drive the van home and Jeanie would be there with a very reasonable explanation. She wrapped the gristle she'd been chewing into her paper serviette as discreetly as she could. Gregory was on the phone behind the bar. She decided not to complain.

After number nine's mum fainted, Joy had driven the van to Sebastopol. Jeanie wasn't there. It would be nonsensical to panic, she told herself, and headed to Ballan. She parked outside the florist's. A woman in her twenties was closing up for the day. No Jeanie.

She drove to Mike's, criss-crossing the rusty car parts on the grass, and knocked on the door. No-one home. She walked around the back and snooped in the windows. Empty. What a relief.

Sebastopol again. No Jeanie, no BMW. It was starting to seem sensible to jump to conclusions – after all, Jeanie only made it two days last time. This was day three. She headed to the old house on the parade. Maybe she was there. Perhaps grief had struck her again. No BMW, no Jeanie. And to her horror Mrs Barnard was on the porch. She saw

Joy in the van and waved some schadenfreude her way. The cemetery. Perhaps she was at the cemetery.

Not there. Exhausted and with low blood sugar, she sat by Bertie's grave, like she did every Sunday after Mass, and said the Our Father and the Hail Mary and asked her husband for strength. This time, she also asked him to forgive her. She had been having some bad thoughts about him for leaving her with nothing. She brushed dry dirt from his plaque and kissed his name. See you Sunday, my darling, she said.

Sebastopol for a third time in as many hours. Jeanie had not returned home. Joy was sickly now, perhaps a little faint, like nine's mum. Her next stop was The Old Smithy. Please Jeanie, do not be there, she thought as she drove to town. Please don't be there.

She wasn't, thankfully. Too early for young drinkers, there were only the die-hard alcoholics at the bar as well as a group of very ill-looking people at the back. The meth users.

Joy stepped back outside. She needed air, and food. She withdrew fifty dollars from the ATM, noticing that her balance had gone down three hundred dollars since yesterday. Jeanie must have used it last night, or this morning. She could hardly walk back into the pub. It was happening again. It had happened again.

'How was your meal?' Gregory asked her.

'It was lovely, Gregory,' Joy said, handing him her plate, which had seven eighths of the steak on it. 'Gregory.' She stopped him before he could race off. 'I was supposed to meet my daughter here.' She showed him the photo of Jeanie that she kept in her wallet. She'd needed it several times in the last two years for the very same reason as this. 'Have you seen her?'

'Yes,' he said. 'She left about an hour ago.'

 ∾

Joy stopped the van in the Bunnings carpark and threw up on the concrete. 'I am so sorry,' she said to the driver parked adjacent.

'No worries,' the tattooed driver said. 'You okay? Can I do anything to help?'

'No, no, but thank you so much.' Her phone beeped. Not Jeanie, but the second-born.

Hey Mrs Salisbury, just wondering if you know where homeless people go?

The driver with the tattoos was still talking to her. 'Don't suppose you do root canals do ya?'

'I'm sorry, the van is my husband's,' she said.

'Does he then? It's killing me.'

'I'm so very sorry, he's dead,' she said.

When she got home, the BMW was in the carport. She raced inside to find Jeanie watching a reality show and eating chips.

'Mum, where have you been?'

'Where have I been? Where have you been?'

'I had a drink at the pub, got waylaid. Sorry, but it's so nice to feel like a free person again.'

Joy fell into the sofa, wiped her nose. 'Just a drink?'

'Yes, just a drink, vodka and tonic – well, three.'

'And you drove your dad's car? You could have killed someone.'

'Jeez, Mum, at least I didn't use.'

'Did you take three hundred dollars out of my account?'

'I did, sorry, I thought I said. I needed clothes for work. I'll give it back payday. Do you want to see what I got?'

'Give me the keys,' Joy said, before noticing they were on the coffee table. She took them, put them in her handbag. 'You're not using the car again.'

'Mum! How am I sposed to get to work?'

'I'll drive you and I'll pick you up.'

'That's dumb. You're over-reacting. Anyway, I can use the van.'

'No you can't,' she said. 'I've promised it to someone else. In fact, I have to go give it to her now.' She might have closed the door with a slight bang. She was having palpita-tions. Once in the van, she texted Camille:

I have a van. You can have that till Friday if you want …
Where are you? I'll come get you.

CHAPTER FIFTEEN

The Mum

Penny had been stalking Andeep from her bed all night and all day. There were two new articles, one in the *Ballarat Courier* and one in *The Age*:

'Andeep Singh, Scottish King of Comedy, Coming to Ballarat To Kick Off His Outrageous New FREEDOM Tour'.

The Ballarat gig was next week. He had several smaller events in Melbourne and Geelong before then. He was looking seriously hot. Penny honed in on his new and expensive-looking headshots. The background was white, blank. Half his face was painted with the Scottish Saltire (yawn, he obviously had not found new subject matter). He was thrusting himself into the very visible bum hole of a blow-up doll. The doll's face was that of the Queen Mother (yawn, was he really going to go on about that ancient blunder of his?) He was wearing *those* jeans. She zoomed in. His hair was coiffed. He had plucked his eyebrows, was wearing eyeliner, mascara too. His skin looked perfect – was that foundation on the other side of his face? Penny had been howling since he walked out, but she had upped the effort since the headshots and the articles.

Penny knew his Facebook password and his email password, and had been refreshing constantly and going through old messages. There was nothing dodgy. He wasn't even Facebook friends with Vanessa. Or he wasn't anymore. He'd probably deleted everything. And he'd probably change his password any moment. Deceitful bastard. She decided to get in first and changed the password herself.

Andeep was only well known in the UK in the nineties, so there was hardly anything online before today. To her horror, though, the Empty Claim YouTube video they did on Saturday had gone viral. The comments were vile. The whole world hated Penny. (*Is this old bat for real? Leave the poor guy alone! #NagHag #PennyIsADog*). And the whole world loved Andeep. (*#YouAreFunnyAndeep #AndeepCanDoBetter #GetOutNowAndeep #SaveAndeep*).

She had his location on Life360. Since the open house Penny had been following his every move. He hadn't gone far – from the Western Inn to Coles to the chippy to the Eureka. Right now he was at the Eureka.

She refreshed her Google search and a new link popped up. Another YouTube video – 'Andeep Singh: THE FREEDOM TOUR'.

It started with the same old 'joke' that lost him his career way back when he apparently had one: involving Prince Phillip taking the Queen Mother up the arse and royal jobby going everywhere. Penny couldn't believe that she actually found this funny the first time. She realised she had stopped crying to actually yawn.

He went on to say it wasn't easy getting cancelled in the nineties and that he would like to apologise for talking in such a manner about the Queen Mother taking it up the arse. 'It's not nice to be mean about dead royals when there are so many alive today. But I am not here to rehash old jokes. I'm here to talk about FREEDOM.'

Here we go, Penny thought. Just as old as the Queen Mother routine. Dead old. He'd get into all the anti-English stuff, how the Scots are way too polite about it all, followed by cheap excrement-related insults.

But the freedom to which Andeep referred was not political. It was personal. It was not freedom from England, it was freedom from Penny.

'My wife didn't find me funny. The truth is, my wife didn't understand me,' he said.

She was getting dizzy. She needed a bucket.

He started speaking in very thick Glaswegian. Even after all these years, Penny could only make out a few words, none of which made her feel better: 'pure hackett'; 'mad minger'; 'aww day bevvy sesh, yaldi'; 'toot toot, chebs oot'. In other circumstances, and if he was referring to someone other than her, she would be laughing. It was funny. No Aussie would understand a word of it. His one-minute taster ended with: 'She kept telling me I'm not funny – every day she told me

– but it was being married to her that was no joke. I am single now, folks. I have declared my independence, and you will hear me shouting from the stages all over this great garden state – FREEDOM!'

A proper roar, it was, up there with Mel – and as he roared, he pointed to the sky, his finger in the plastic bum hole of the Queen Mother.

Penny threw up. Red-wine bile went all over the mezzanine floor.

Andeep had found some new material.

CHAPTER SIXTEEN

The Second-Born

The serenity was short-lived, DD. I woke to my Facebook Messenger going off loudly and intensely, over and over, the same half-second between each BEEP. My volume wasn't even set high. It had to be Asha. Even her message beeps felt like oi stabs. Now I have unfriended her on Facebook as well as blocking her phone number. But there are so many ways for her to get in touch, and I just know she will find one of them.

The Great Ocean Road doesn't seem great after the lengthy essay she sent in parts so I wouldn't forget to keep reading. I wish I hadn't read it. My head is splitting, and now I know I have to drive back to Ballarat and face the really terrible music.

I have forgiven you.

That's how her message started. Seriously, she has forgiven me. If my jaw wasn't so sore I'd guffaw.

And I won't ask you again what happened in Geelong. You are obviously determined to hide it from me, for reasons I can't and won't ever understand. I am going to move on.

For two paragraphs or so it was like notes from my English professor – nice thing, nice thing, nice thing ... eg:

I love you, Camille. You are my little sister. When you started secondary school I used to come and see if you were okay every single lunch time. I never once ignored you like Natasha Gregg et al ignored and bullied their little sisters. I used to read you stories when you were small, every single night, because you were scared to go to sleep. I made you fit and healthy. I made you go for jogs, do stretches, practise your throws. You would never have that netball trophy if not for me.

What netball trophy?

Beep.

When I left for uni you told me I was your best friend, you cried your eyes out. You said I would be your maid of honour.

Niceties done, her 'notes' moved on to the real shizzle, which is how shite I am. This time, Asha's disappointments included:

That I lied to her. She didn't think I would ever lie to her: *We are sisters. We are each other's shared historians, like the therapist said. We will be each other's longest relationship in life. We have loyalty, do we not? Can't you see how upset I am, don't you care?*

My longest relationship, oh lord. Her list went on:

You know how in love I am. That Richard is THE ONE.

Beep.

He is the love of my life. You wouldn't understand. You've never been in love, but one day you might fall for someone and he might fall for you and you will feel bad about the way you've treated me. You must know I'm in agony not hearing anything, knowing he's there with his wife when he should be with me; that she has jailed me here – that's right, SHE did it. Richard would never have called the police and insisted on an interdict and all this bullshit just because we had an argument, just because of the coffee incident.

'Coffee incident', ha! She threw a tamper at him, those things are heavier than hammers, he had to get stitches. They could have done her for attempted murder. She was very lucky not to go to jail.

I just can't handle it. I've been stuck here, Camille, for two weeks. I haven't seen my friends. I haven't been to church, and you know Dance Said He is everything to me now. I haven't kissed him. I haven't heard his voice telling me I am the one, I am the one. I am his. I haven't even had long gorgeous messages from him, so beautiful, you wouldn't believe the things he says to me. I know I lashed out…

I thought she was going to say she lashed out at me. I thought she was going to apologise for bruising me all over and making me run for my life. NO.

…at him because I was so upset. But I understand he couldn't stop Rowena reporting me. He had to keep her on side, he had to keep a public face on. He didn't want me on this ankle bracelet. It was her. But you probably heard differently, yeah? She probably gave you a whole other story, and there was no way for him to back me up. He is going to come to me. He is

going to be mine again. We have plans. We have definite plans. I am working at it. He is working at it. And you won't even tell me what they said. And I won't ever ask you. But where is the empathy? Where is the love? Where is sisterhood?

Beep.

You don't show me love, you lie to me. You withhold information that I desperately want and need and you don't seem to care. How can you lie to me? Why are you being so hurtful?

Beep.

… … … … … And …

Beep.

…Since I left home, you hardly ever called me, you never visited me. I had to drop out of uni! I had to get a basic shitty job in the city! I've been sharing a house with friends who won't even let me stay there on this tag – the court asked and they said no. How do you think it felt coming back here with shackles on? Leaving my job and my flat and the love of my life and the church that I need so badly? How do you think I've been feeling? YOU DON'T CARE. I am so alone.

Beep.

And now you are deceiving me. I am so upset, Camille. I am sobbing here. I can see you are reading this. Nothing? You're not even typing? Really?

After the professorial niceties, which eased me into the disappointments that I must address, the message focused on inducing guilt and, obviously, the favours I must do.

But I love you. I always will. You are my sister. We are bound together forever. Still nothing? I know you are reading.

Beep.

I suppose you know about Dad? He has left for good. He wants a divorce. Mum is going to Uncle James's first thing in the morning, he's coming to get her, before court tomorrow. She wants to know if you will take me to court. She wants to know that you will take me to the train after, see I get back to Sunshine safe and sound. She wants to know that my sister will look after me. And I can't tell her the truth, that I have no idea if you will help me, if you give one tiny shit about me. Do you love me? Am I your sister?

Beep.

Mum is utterly devastated. I've been rubbing her feet and ordering home deliveries and we've run out of money. Nothing, nada, in the bank. Mum can't even pay the mortgage and the electricity, and Dad isn't answering her calls or even mine. She can't move off the bed, and I can't go out. She really needs you to get some shopping for her. You do understand I can't go out? That if I leave the house I will go to jail.

Beep.

Dad's bad-mouthing her all over the internet. She's being trolled. I can't believe it. I could murder him. We should do something, don't you think? I think one of us...

(ie, me)

...should at least go and give him a talking to, you must

*agree? So anyway I am not going to ask what Richard and
Rowena said. I'm going to try and move on. And I have forgiven
you. My hope is that you might let Jesus into your heart. He has
really helped me.*

Hahaha, my whole face aches.

*If you can't find it in your heart to take me to court it will be
the last thing I ask of you, if that is what you want. If it's not
what you want, if you want a sister, then it is your turn to show
me the sisterhood. Your turn to check on me. Your turn to call
me. Your turn to visit me. Your turn to make some effort,
Camille, because we are...*

BEEEEEP!

∼

It's hours later, DD. Asha's Facebook essay sent me into a
guilt tail-spin for quite a while. I had to go for a swim and
a run to work through it. I had to keep reminding myself:
she'll be gone tomorrow, she'll be gone. Even though she
won't be in the house anymore, I know I have to leave too.
I can't help Mum, she is beyond help. I don't want to help.
I've decided I am going to go to WA. I'm gonna head to
Ballarat now and ask Dad for some money, not much, just
enough for bills and food for Mum – and for a one-way
ticket to Perth. I'm going to go to the mines and be a truck
driver or a cleaner or a housekeeper or a bartender. I might

live in a hostel and make lots of friends from faraway places, and they'll invite me to stay with them in Zurich or Capetown or Hanoi. I might live underground, or above a scary pub with beardy men who'll call me a bird or a slut, but I won't care cos I'll be making a fortune and I'll be in WA, so wonderfully far away. I'll work then I'll travel then I'll work then I'll travel. I am so excited about it. All I need is a ticket, and they're practically free. I'm getting out of here. I'm gonna take the van back to Mrs S tomorrow and then I'm gonna go. I've never been so excited. I should have done this months ago.

First, the dosh from Dad. I am not telling him off like Asha wants. I'm not murdering him. I've looked at his new headshots and his new video, and he looks so happy. He's really funny. Apart from bumming the ticket money, I am just gonna leave Dad be. Good on him. I'm happy for him. I'll drop off food and money for Mum. I will not talk to Asha. She will not draw me back in.

Seeya, DD, off to Ballarat. Might stay in one of those lovely spots on the Werribee tonight, one final hurrah in this ace dental chair. Must buy Mrs S a thank-you pressie. I am so happy!

∽

Sorry my writing's shaky. It's nearly midnight. I didn't make it to the Werribee river. I'm about twenty minutes out of town under a bridge. It's not pretty but I think it's safe. Dad was at the Eureka, discussing stuff with a bunch of people. It's probably best if we don't watch Dad's new sets tbh, especially Mum. Comedians always write what they know. Vanessa was there. I wasn't not-nice to her, but I didn't feel like being nice either. It's all so icky. Everything seems so different and dark and dangerous. Dad's got gigs all over the place in the next few weeks, which is great news for him. He's off to Melbourne today, won't be back till next week. He gave me enough money for Mum to get by another month and asked me to take care of her and Asha. I can't believe what I said – I said I would, of course I would. Then I bought a ticket to Perth straight away – I leave from Tullamarine on Saturday. I will care for the two of them until they go tomorrow. One more day, DD, one more day. I can do that. The day after that I am gone. I don't know why I'm not buzzing like I was last night, I should be. I am going to another state, I am going to be another person. I am gonna have another life.

After seeing Dad, I bought a whole stack of food and some shortbread and a card for Mrs S. I parked a block from the house and handwrote a very carefully crafted note to Asha, hoping to leave it without having to speak to her:

I will take you to court tomorrow. I'll collect you at 9.30. I will take you to the train straight after.
Cam x

I went to the house, snuck round the back, left the note and the bags of food on the kitchen bench and tiptoed upstairs to see Mum.

There's no window in that horrible mezzanine, and the room smelt of cigarette smoke, which Mum had obviously decided to take up since I left. She must have made it to the shops somehow, or she had a secret stash in the house. She was sleeping in the same tight dress she had on when I last saw her. Her sheets were wet with sweat and tears and maybe even urine. Several bottles of pills were open on the bedside table – diazepam, sertraline, paracetamol. Asha may well have been massaging her feet and brushing her hair but she'd done bugger all else.

'Mum? Wakey wakey,' I said as quietly as I could. I did not want Asha to hear me.

'Cammy,' she slurred. She'd had too much diazepam, I think. I checked the paracetamol bottle – nearly full. Thank god she hadn't tried anything stupid. Just in case, I emptied most of the pills and put them in my pocket.

'Hey Mum, you wee soul.' I lifted her tiny body, hugged her, holding my nose. 'I'm getting you in the shower.'

She sniffed and it made her cry. 'I stink and your dad

doesn't love me anymore. Cammy, he doesn't love me, he doesn't love me, can you believe that? I have to say it over and over, he doesn't love me, he doesn't love me.'

'You should stop saying it over and over,' I said. 'You don't need him, you don't need him to love you.' I scraped her dress off her, added it to the pile of washing in the corner. 'You need food and a shower.'

'And a drink?' she said.

'There isn't any alcohol,' I lied. There were two goon sacks of wine in my secret hiding spot. 'Anyway, it'd make you feel worse, you know that.'

'I do know that, what a pathetic, sad case I am. My name is Penny and I stink and I'm unlovable and I'm an alcoholic.' She popped a diazepam, downed it dry.

I helped her to the ensuite and turned on the shower. She held her hands against the tiles, her head hanging low, tears etcetera dribbling from her nose and her open mouth. I'd never seen her naked and up close like this, but it was only weird for a few seconds. After that, it was all about the flannel and the suds. She did not stop crying as I wrapped her in towels and sat her up in bed. 'Take this,' I said, handing her the hair dryer. 'I'll be back with sustenance. Hold it up, don't point it at your face, it's for your hair, ya dill!'

I could hear music and chanting coming from Asha's room. Phew, she was preoccupied, raising the dead, chatting to Gee-suss. I was able to heat tomato soup, butter some toast and slice an apple without her hearing me. I found one of Mum's floral decoupage trays and added an icy OJ and a cup of tea. So pretty and comforting, the kind of tray Mum used to make for me when I was a child and she was a parent.

'You are my little baby girl,' she said, crying as I spooned soup into her droopy mouth, pushed in tiny squares of toast. 'My little baby, my youngest. Do you think I'm ugly? Do you love me?'

'You're way better-looking than Vanessa,' I said, meaning it. 'And I love you to bits. Of course I do.' I gave her a sip of OJ, another square of toast. 'You're an inspiration, not right now obviously, but usually.'

'Your dad doesn't think so. He thinks I'm a piece of old rubbish.'

The diazepam was making her sleepy, her eyes were closing.

'You need rest. You are going to feel so much better after a good sleep. You are going to get over this. I know you – you're going to make plans and you are going to thrive.' I took the damp towels off and replaced them with a cotton nightie.

'My disgusting old-lady nightie,' she said, 'perfect, because that's what I am.'

'You are not disgusting, you are beautiful and you are not old, you're in your prime. You're just sad, Mum, but you won't be for long. Everything's going to be okay. You are going to feel better so soon.'

'James is coming to get me in the morning,' she said.

'See? You've already made plans. That's great.'

'He's the best brother.'

I thought she was asleep. I was about to gather everything up and head off. She grabbed my hand, eyes still closed. 'Promise me you'll look after Asha.'

My stomach sank. I said nothing for ages.

She opened her eyes. 'I always wanted two children. I hated the idea of Asha being on her own. Only children are so lonely. And annoying. Men are bastards, Cammy, utter dicks. I am so glad you have each other, my babies, my little girls.'

Oh Jeez Jeez Jeez. 'I'm going to take her to court tomorrow,' I said. 'I'm going to make sure she gets back to Melbourne safe and sound.'

'You promise?'

'I promise.'

❧

I almost made it out of the house. So close. But the rubbish bin lid shut really loudly and before I could slide the glass door open Asha was behind me.

'Where are you going?' she said, reading the note I'd left, which did not seem to please her.

'I'm not staying here tonight,' I said. 'I'll see you in the morning.'

'Okay, fine,' she said, 'thanks for doing the shopping.' She started emptying the first of the three shopping bags I'd left: linguine, eggs, pancetta, cream, Parmesan. She took things out, one by one, her face getting redder and tighter with each item – lettuce, bread, garlic, butter, grapes, goats cheese, cucumber, ice-cream.

'Carbonara again?' she said.

'There's also a free-range chicken and spuds and greens in one of the other bags, if you'd prefer.'

She looked in the second bag (which had orange juice, apples, Vegemite, jam, croissants, coffee, baked beans); then in the third, which had the makings of roast chicken. 'Where's the wine?'

'I forgot,' I said.

'You forgot?'

'Yes.'

'Like you forgot to tell me you spent a whole day with my boyfriend.'

I was starting to lose my cool. 'And his wife,' I said.

'So you admit it now, you did spend the whole day with them.'

Fuck it, I thought, the Rs were even crazier than she was, why did I owe them a promise?

'Yeah, I spent the whole day with them, first at the prayer

meeting, then at the house. I had lunch with them. I had a snooze in their backyard. They drove me home. They told me how you're trying to bring their dead kid back to life. "Rise Nellie Rise! I want to see your smiley face, I want to push you on the swing." Fucking whack-job that you are.'

'Gee-suss is a whack job too then, hey? He didn't heal, he didn't raise Lazarus from the grave? We shrunk her tumour! We shrunk her tumour! God is crazy is He, the Bible is crazy, the power of prayer is crazy, faith and love is crazy?'

'Um, yeah.'

'You're going to go to Hell.'

'I am looking forward to it. But first I will take you to court and I will take you to the train because you are a complete loser who can't do anything for yourself. You are dangerous and violent, and I am sick of you. I don't want anything to do with you after that. I am leaving on Saturday. I never want to see you again.'

She picked up the note I'd left, scrutinising it. 'So this note you left – this note you signed with your affectionate pet name, the name I call you when we're happy – *Cam* – and this kiss at the bottom, is just more lies.'

I thought I'd written something succinct and safe. I forgot how an innocently insincere 'dear' or 'love' could provoke my sister. She'd ripped up several birthday cards due to hypocritical wording. She'd hurled many ill-considered gifts in the bin. She'd ended two friendships due to disingenuous punctuation.

'Yes, yes more lies. The kiss is a lie, it is meaningless. It does not mean that I actually want to kiss you. It does not mean that I actually love you. And the *Cam*, that was an attempt to seem calm and loving in order to stop you from strangling me again, or head-butting me again, or punching me in the head again, or smashing me in the back with a phone again or breaking my nose with a netball again.'

'You whiney little prat. We were doing passes and you can't catch. What kind of sister wants to make me look bad in front of Mum and Dad and the therapist, and god knows who else you've bad-mouthed me to. Broke your nose! All you do is lie. Meanwhile, you have left me here with her' – she pointed upstairs – 'and I can't get out. Meanwhile you've spent hours and hours with my boyfriend.'

'Who is married. Seemed very happy to me. They seemed into each other. They didn't stop touching the whole time I was with them, holding hands, walking arm in arm, kissing. When I was having a rest I heard them doing it in the bedroom. She definitely came. He says the nicest things to her. He calls her Ro-Ro. Says she's his best friend, the love of his life, his meaning, his everything. He had his hand on her leg the whole way from Geelong to Ballarat. He loves her so much. He calls you his indiscretion, his big mistake, his great regret. They think you're a loose cannon, Asha, they both think you're as crazy as I think you are. He doesn't want anything to do with you. They made me promise not to tell you anything. They never want to see you again, especially Richard.'

'You are making all that up.'

'Am I?' (Not all of it, but quite a portion. It felt good.)

'You're cruel, you're evil. You're a selfish little narcissist. You take take take and you lie lie lie.'

'Well I'm not going to lie anymore. You are unwell. You are unhinged. You need help. You're dangerous. You terrify me.'

'I terrify you! Who's the one with all the power here? Who's the one taunting?'

'You are out of control and bat-shit crazy, and I will take you to court tomorrow because I have promised Mum and Dad I will, and I will see you get on the train to Sunshine, not because I promised, although I did, but because I want to make sure you get out of this town and out of my life.'

She threw an egg at me. It burst on my forehead, dribbled down my face. Not reacting to this – bar licking salmonella from my lip – caused her to throw another item my way, the tub of single cream this time, which oozed all over my hair and my face, and dribbled all over my top. I licked some of that too. Before I knew it she had thrown the pancetta and the parmesan and the goats cheese and the cucumber at me. I didn't move, I stood still, a target.

'Asha, is that you?' Mum said from upstairs.

'Yes Mum,' she replied, nicey nicey, before throwing the

free-range chicken at my head. I ducked and it bounced off the stone wall. Time to leave.

A few things hit my back before I shut the glass door behind me and made it outside into the courtyard. Just in time, as she hurled a can of baked beans in my direction. The door shattered, glass ricocheted everywhere, spraying my back. Shards landed in my carbonara hair, several pierced my arms. With blood everywhere, I ran out the back gate to the carpark and into the van.

CHAPTER SEVENTEEN

The Therapist

Joy didn't know anyone who had any fun after the age of eighty. Mrs Benson from the begonia festival had to get rails all over the house at seventy-nine. She had an enormous plastic shower cubicle with rails everywhere that made Joy feel dirty and sad when she saw it. As for poor Mrs Rogers and her rheumatoid arthritis – she was getting shorter and curlier every time Joy saw her. And Claire McConaughey, just seventy-eight, she couldn't get insurance to go to Los Angeles even though she had the COPD well under control. After all those years saving for the big trip, to be let down like that, to be unable to see her great-grandchild in the flesh. Joy spotted Claire in the mall a few weeks ago buying bulk kitchen roll at the reject shop. She definitely was not having any fun.

Joy would not be crestfallen about the bail money she would need to pay the following day, probably thousands, perhaps thousands and thousands. She'd already spoken to a few companies and could release equity from her home immediately. It was very easy and such a relief. Money from the house could cover a fine too, and compensation, if that was necessary. She'd do whatever she could to save Jeanie from going to jail. She wasn't down about the BMW either. She did not need the fancy car. She did not need to smell Bertie's disinfectant. It would be best not to be reminded of Bertie all the time. It was better without his suits and without his enormous furniture. The BMW stood out in her new suburb anyway, and she didn't like that. She didn't want to rub money in other people's faces. Such good people too. Everyone she'd met since the move was friendly and caring. Giorgio and Amanda at Bertolini's Café were just wonderful, remembering her name every single time and that she liked her coffee hotter than it should be and with a lot of froth. She was glad to have left the parade. The only person to have been in touch since the move was Anne McLean, who had left a message that afternoon:

Hello, Joy, Anne here, the message said. *I looked up the building you enquired about. You got the spelling wrong, silly. It's JE Collins, not JB. An easy mistake, it's quite weathered after all these years. 1895, a truly remarkable piece of history. It was a wine merchant's. I found some old plans in the archives and will post them through your letterbox on the way home from my meetings. Please keep them safe and return asap, they are originals. Best, Anne.*

The envelope came through the letterbox two hours after the message, no attempt at a knock. She heard Anne's tyres screech. Joy expected a new-home card to be included with the post. Alas, just ancient original plans of the Moloney-Singh home, which had been a wine merchant's, JE Collins, established 1895. The original deeds showed it to be one large, high-ceilinged warehouse. The only surprise being that there was a wine cellar underneath. Looked like it must be under the pottery-wheel room – Camille's bedroom now. Joy didn't notice a hatch when she was at the open house. Interesting.

She was mad with Anne McLean. Her message didn't include any niceties: 'hope the move went well' or 'how is your daughter? or 'how are you?' It was a little saddening to learn that no-one cared about her in Ballarat, in Victoria, in Australia. Even Jeanie didn't, she was beginning to let herself think, even Jeanie didn't love her. How she missed home. How she longed to be in England. It had always been the plan. Bertie had promised. When they retired, he would follow her this time. They would move to England, to the green fields and the crisp winters and the muddy walks and the over-the-top Christmases and the peaceful and fun and perfect and unconditional love of her little sister, Rosie.

She didn't care about the BMW, but it was best not to think of how it happened. Jeanie taking it the very night Joy had banned her from using it, stealing the keys from her handbag while she was sleeping and setting off without her knowledge. It was 4am Friday morning when the police came to the door.

'Are you Mrs Salisbury?' the police officer said.

She nodded. The palpitations had never been so loud.

'Is your daughter Jean Salisbury?'

'Yes,' she said, holding her hand over her heart.

'And you are the owner of a 1994 black BMW, registered NPR 786?'

'Yes.' Oh dear God, Jeanie is dead, Jeanie is dead, *Our Father who art in heaven, hallowed...*

'Did you give your daughter permission to drive the car?'

Oh thank god, she might be alive ... *hallowed be thy name, thy kingdom come, thy will be done...*

'Mrs Salisbury? I asked you if you gave your daughter permission to drive the vehicle? She had taken the plates off, we are guessing you didn't.'

Joy didn't know the best answer in this instance. She hadn't added Jeanie to the insurance – she had forgotten. How could she have let her drive to Ballan? She was so silly, so forgetful. Hence, if she said yes, both of them would be in trouble. But if she said no, that she had not given permission, perhaps this would land Jeanie in bigger trouble. She could be charged with stealing the car. After a very brief pause, Joy decided on the truth. The truth had worked for her for seventy-one years, she was not about to change that now. 'No, I didn't give her permission,' she said. 'I didn't even know she'd taken it. I've been asleep.'

'The car has been confiscated.'

So she might be alive. Thank you, lord, thank you, Jesus, thank you. 'Confiscated?'

'Yes, confiscated. You'll get a letter. She's in jail. Court today on anti-hoon laws. Four priors and this vehicle has been impounded on three occasions in the last two years – are you aware of this? Or you don't remember?'

She remembered, now she did.

'No plates, no licence, no insurance, tested positive for methamphetamine, alcohol, cannabis. She drove through two red lights, 120k in a sixty zone, nearly ran over an elderly gentlemen in Lydiard Street, coulda killed the poor old bastard. Kept driving like a maniac – how old is she?'

'She's forty-three.'

'Forty-three! Ended up smashing into the Boer War Memorial, that's gonna cost her, there's gonna be compensation for that. She's lucky to be alive, but I'm not sure the rest of us are lucky she is. She won't be driving again, ever. And if she's lucky enough to avoid jail she'll be looking at a humdinger of a fine, plus compensation for the damage to the flower beds round the monument. She's not going to be popular round here, bashing that. My great-grandfather was one of the 238 who fell for our Empire. Makes my stomach churn, that does, junkie hoon, she should be pruning roses at her age.' He shook his head at Joy, tut-tutting her parenting.

෴

Joy arrived at the court at ten to ten, surprised to see number nine's first- and second-borns waiting out the front beside the dental van. She greeted them with a smile, but it was only the second-born who managed to smile back.

'Mrs S! I have a pressie for you. Your van saved my life, thank you thank you. You are the best person I have ever met.'

She gave Joy a huge hug. It felt unbelievably good to be hugged.

'What are you doing here?' she asked. 'I was going to bring it to you straight after this. Well, I'm taking Asha to the train, then I was going to. Do you want the keys now? I can walk Asha to the train. She doesn't have much stuff, it's so close.'

'Thank you,' Joy said. 'Did you enjoy van life?'

'I LOVED van life,' she said, grabbing Asha's small suitcase and the shortbread out of the van and giving her the keys and the present. 'It's probably the most comfortable I've ever been. You could live in it, you know, has everything you need. Feels free, there are so many beautiful places to go.'

I'll probably have to, Joy thought, what with the money she was going to have to lash out to keep Jeanie out of jail, including another ten grand for rehab. The first-born seemed unwell, shaky, white as a ghost.

'You okay, honey?' she said, stroking Asha's arm.

'Nervous. Just can't wait to get this thing off.'

'No need for nerves, is there?'

'Hope not.'

Second-born rolled her eyes.

'My lawyer says this'll be the end of it. But I'm still worried. What if the judge is mean? If I can't go back to work, I'll lose my job, they won't hold it for me another month. I've got no holidays left. I had to use all my holidays, some break! And I'll lose my rental too, although my house-mates haven't been very nice. I'll look for something else soon as I can, I reckon. It's been hard.'

Joy gave the poor girl a hug. She was a mess. 'I'll say a prayer for you.'

'Please do,' she said, cheered by the offer. 'I'd really appreciate that.'

&

Joy headed off to a different court from the girls, shaky and scared, saying two Hail Marys on the way for Asha. She'd been to court with a few of her clients in the past but had never had to go for a member of her own family. When Jeanie arrived in cuffs and took her seat at the front her heart started doing its thing. She held her hand over it. How had it come to this, a prosecutor speaking about her daughter with callousness, likening her to all the other meth users in town, calling her a hoon and a junkie and a danger to society? Joy blew her nose too loudly. She put her head down to get some blood back into it. Jeanie was pleading not guilty. The judge was not pleased.

Her phone buzzed. Rosie.

She wasn't supposed to have her phone in court. She wasn't supposed to look at it, but the prosecutor was still talking about an alien, not her daughter, and she couldn't listen.

It was the twenty-third text. Ten missed calls. She only read the most recent:

☹

That was all.

They were talking about bail at the front of the court. Twenty-thousand dollars was being mentioned. She was a flight risk, the prosecutor said, as well as high risk of causing imminent harm. To stay out of jail before trial, someone would need to cough up. Joy was about to be twenty thousand dollars poorer, for a while at least.

She was finding it hard to sit still. Her shoulders were shaking. She could hardly hold the phone.

If only Rosie was sitting here, holding her hand. If only they could walk out of here together. Joy let herself drift into the fantasy.

She and Rosie drive off in the van. They take turns at the wheel, with the music blaring. Uncool music. Country music. They're singing at the top of their lungs. They're eating carefully selected snacks. They're letting the breeze blow through the windows, through their hair, they're marvelling at the fields and the rivers and the mountains.

At the front of the court, the lawyers were discussing a trial date. It would be in three weeks. By then, Joy would be another ten thousand dollars poorer because she will have paid for a fourth rehab. Better to escape to Rosie.

They're in the van. They're looking for the perfect place to eat the perfect lunch. It's a kitsch café with strawberry milkshakes in battered metal cups with cream on top. They're walking with water bottles and chocolate bars, not needing to talk, each with earphones in, breathing in, taking in the beauty. At night they make a fire by a river or on a beach. They set up the camping table and cook yummy things and enjoy every second of it. They go to sleep in the van in soft sheets and bouncy duvets and say night night and…

Up front, they were talking about sentencing options. If Jeanie was lucky and got a fine instead of jail Joy would be another twelve thousand dollars poorer, plus compensation for damage to the memorial. Joy couldn't afford mortgage re-payments at this level. Even in Ballarat there weren't enough unhappy families to pay for this. She would need to do more than release equity from her tiny Sebastopol unit. She would need to sell it. She would need to paint the van and live in it.

Was it really always so perfect with Rosie? Joy might be rewriting history. She went back over the trips they'd had:

London, 2004, they stayed in a hotel in Bloomsbury and wandered the streets all day long, in and out of pubs and museums and department stores. At night they ate in Soho or in Chinatown – yes, that was perfect.

Cornwall, 2005. Afternoons reading newspapers in old pubs with log fires overlooking cliffs and waves. Ahhh.

Leeds and Liverpool Canal, 2006. Unbeatably, impossibly perfect.

After each trip, Joy cried all the way to Singapore, apologising to the poor passenger next to her and using an unprecedent number of the hankies Rosie ironed for her.

Argyll, 2007. She had never experienced such beauty; had never laughed so hard.

The farewells at the airport each time were the same – dreadful, stomach-churning tears. And then plans. We will go to Brighton next June. See you in Liverpool next September. I will book my ticket on the plane. I will send you the itinerary as soon as I get home.

Joy texted back:

That was all.

She would never be moving home. She would probably never see England again. She wouldn't even get to see Rosie next month. She would not meet her at Heathrow. She would not be greeted at arrivals with a squeal, a scream – and a huge, embarrassing sign that said *JOY TO THE WORLD*. There would not be an energetic, optimistic, happy, life-loving woman running towards her, arms open, beautifully styled and with a smile as wide and as white as the one on the van. She would not be hugged and loved, and she would not hear her little sister, her best friend, the love of her life, say something like:

'Holy shizzle, girl, I am throwing out those trousers as soon as we get home. You look like a bag lady. Where did you get them, the tip? What were you thinking?'

She would not be driven to Rosie's beautiful cottage, which she would have spent days and days perfecting, the gorgeous garden, fairy lighting on the trees and around the pond, favourite English foods, soft, ironed bedding, a bottle of wine or two. They would not send Rosie's husband to bed and dance in the kitchen, two old ladies, two old ladies who loved each other and promised each other always to dance. Rosie, she could not go and see Rosie.

The date for trial was set, the bail agreed. Joy texted again:

Jeanie has relapsed. The car is gone. I have to sell the unit. I am going to live in the dental van. I can't come. I love you so much. I am so sorry.

As Jeanie's cuffs were released, Joy managed to lift her head. She probably wouldn't get travel insurance anyway, like Claire McConaughey. Theses palpitations were relentless. She probably had something terrible, like a heart condition that would probably prohibit her from flying all the way to the U.K. anyway. Twenty-one hours on a plane. The thought was making her nauseous. No-one she knew enjoyed travelling in their seventies anyway. This was okay, this was all right. She would talk to Rosie on the phone every few days. She would ring her straight after court and they would make plans. Weekly Zooms. Handwritten letters. Old-fashioned phone calls. They would find a way to keep loving each other. She texted Rosie again:

I am going to find a way for it to be okay. I love you.

CHAPTER EIGHTEEN

The Second-Born

I've done something v bad. I can hardly write, it's unreadable. My hand, I think it might be broken. Prob good if I stop.

I am going to try my left hand.

It is impossible.

That took me an hour.

That was a waste of a sentence.

I am drinking wine.

Ah, better now. Drink and paracetamol. I can write with my right hand again. Gotta tell you what I've done, and tbh it's not seeming so bad anymore. I think there are worse things I could have done. I think there are worse things I will do if she doesn't stop that banging.

કં

I made it all the way from the house to the court without saying a word to Asha. Thankfully she didn't try talking to me either. Her freedom was within reach. She was about to get her tag removed, she was about to be allowed to leave. I think she was planning to go straight to Richard and get him back. She didn't look happy as such, but she wasn't foaming with rage like she usually is. Come to think of it, she might have been praying to herself. That's probably it, she was probs saying: dear god, let Richard be mine again, let him be mine. She was probably planning a giant resurrection event with Richard, or at least an erection one. It's actually all that matters to her. Not Gee-suss or god or the holy ghost or heaven or dead Nellie, just The Dick. I was planning my WA trip in my head. And then we went inside and saw the two Rs talking to the lawyers in the corridor and both of us nearly fainted.

'Richard, Richard,' she yelled. She ran towards him. 'Richard!'

He didn't even look at her, or at me. He held Rowena's hand and they scurried into the court and took a seat at the front with the prosecutor. I was offended, which is weird. Why hadn't either of them looked at me either?

'Why are they here?' she kept saying.

Despite feeling a tad on her side, for the first time in weeks, I didn't respond. I was still determined not to speak to her again. The judge hushed the court and she whispered:

'What are they saying up there?'

When I didn't respond she pushed against my arm with hers. I pushed back against it. Our pushes got harder, our whole bodies were involved. If one of us had stopped the other would have been bowled over.

'What are they whispering? Oi!'

She pinched my arm this time, no poke. It hurt so much I almost said something really loudly that would not have been appropriate in court.

'What's going on, you know something, don't you?'

They called her up to the naughty chair and everything went from bad to worse. The prosecutor outlined her breaches – she had attempted to make contact with the victim by phone on 112 occasions; via her Facebook account on twelve occasions and on a fake Facebook account on thirty-six occasions. Her sister had harassed the pastor and his wife – going so far as to visit their place of worship. She then followed them to their house to beg for information and contact. But the worst thing, the clincher, was that Asha had left our house illegally, breaching the conditions of her electronic monitoring, then visited the grave of their dead child, where she lay on the tomb and disturbed the earth around it. Desecrated. She had desecrated little Nellie's grave. She was a monster.

Yes, yes, I thought, she is a monster, but not for those reasons.

Before I knew it they were talking about further assessments – a three-week period during which she would need alcohol counselling and a mental-health assessment. This could either take place on remand or at home with the ankle bracelet.

Remand, I was thinking, remand.

It took a moment for me to realise the lawyers and the judge were asking me something. Was the family willing to have her in the home again?

Asha was giving me a look I hadn't seen for weeks (and not very often before then when I come to think of it): sad, pathetic, vulnerable. I liked it. 'Please, please,' she mouthed from the naughty chair.

Could I really say no and send her to jail? So tempting. The answer to my prayers in fact.

Richard and Rowena both gave me scathing looks. I was scum like Asha. Stalking scum. And at that moment I hated the two of them more than I hated Asha. They had started the whole Rise Nellie thing. They were liars. They were deranged brainwashers. It wasn't Asha's fault.

'Yes,' I said. 'I am her sister and I live at the address and I agree to having her there.'

Asha didn't try to talk to Richard again. She walked right by them and out of the court. Something had changed in her.

We walked back to the house together, not saying a word.

My arm was red from the pinch, and although I was filled with rage about the two Rs and had agreed to help her in court, I did not intend to communicate with her ever again.

As we walked past the shops she said: 'He doesn't love me.'

Poor Asha. She had finally realised. I could feel the despair in my tummy too.

'I want to kill him,' she said.

I understood.

'Promise you'll stop me killing him,' she said.

I kept walking. I would not be drawn in.

'Camille, please, promise me you won't let me kill him?'

Fuck, I was going to have to speak. 'I promise,' I said.

'Have you got any money? Can we get booze?'

'Can you buy me some wine? I need to get drunk.'

Kept walking. Mouth zipped.

'I haven't got any money. Can you give me some money please?' she said. 'I'll go in and get it.'

I didn't give her money, didn't say a word. My escape to an underground mine in Western Australia was no longer. I was stuck here again, making promises. I could hardly believe it had happened.

'Did you tell Richard I was at the cemetery?'

Don't say a word, Cam, not a word. Even though I hadn't told them. Must have been the cops. I can do this, I repeated to myself, I'll do these three weeks, but I will not speak to her.

'You despise me, don't you? All you want is to hurt me.'

I walked faster. Just get home, just get to the house and into your room, I was thinking. I was a few feet ahead of her.

Suddenly I felt her shove my back. I catapulted forward and did a slow-motion fall that I tried to break with my hand – in doing so I think I actually broke my hand. It's doubled in size. I have a huge graze on my hand and on my knee. I can't walk properly. I nearly landed on my face. A middle-aged couple saw what happened, but they said nothing. They smiled at each other and walked on by. 'Takes me back,' one was probably recalling affectionately to the other. 'My sister pushed me off a ladder once.'

I upped the pace, got to the front door and inside. 'There's wine in my room,' I said.

'I knew it.' She ran to my room, rummaged through my clothes, through my drawers, under my duvet. 'Where?'

It was time to divulge my secret hiding place. I moved the faux sheepskin covered gym mat, exposing the huge bluestones underneath.

Unimpressed at the bare flooring, she readied herself to throttle me. I wondered how she'd do it this time, with her fists, with a sculpting tool, with the screwdriver?

'There's a cellar under here,' I said, kneeling down and retrieving the flat screwdriver I had hidden under my pillow since changing rooms. I levered the crack and one of the huge heavy stones moved. I prised it open until it was leaning against the wall. It was a hatch.

'Oh my god,' she said, looking down into the dark hole.

I put my phone torch on to illuminate the ladder, and I

went down first. I'd made it quite pleasant in the last few days. I lit the gas lamp Mum found in a skip behind the Methodist church and a few of the candles we'd failed to sell at the open house. The two goon sacks of dry red were sitting on one of the three beautiful wooden barrels, and so were you, DD. I put you down my jeans while she was wandering around, wowing. It was tempting not to tell her about the mine shaft in the corner.

BTW, the mine shaft is HUGE, about six by six feet. The earth around it is all soft – looks like the shaft was covered and hidden and has just recently opened up on its own. I've dropped bottles down there and didn't even hear them smash. The local mine shaft chasers would come in their pants. So dangerous. Probably why the cellar has been closed off and kept secret.

I decided I'd better let Asha know.

'Be careful in the corner,' I said. 'Must be an old claim. Goes down for miles.'

She was checking out the dusty bottles of ancient wine on the wooden shelves. There were six altogether. 1895. Good enough for her.

The cellar was half the size of the property. I discovered it when we moved rooms. Sleeping on the floor, as I was forced to do, I noticed a draft coming through the crack and took a closer look. When Asha was busy praying and singing I'd jam the bedroom door with the desk and open it up. It had been my escape, I loved it. I had water and biccies and a few books down there too, which was lucky, because I had an idea. A really good one.

'I'll go get some glasses, shall I?' I grabbed one of the goon sacks of dry red and walked back up the ladder. I could hear Asha popping a cork and laughing.

'This actually tastes okay – like caramel!'

Then I slammed the bluestone hatch down again.

'Hey, hey!' she yelled. 'What are you doing?' She was knocking at it from underneath, trying to push it. 'Hey, are you kidding me?'

She probably couldn't move the stone. It weighed a ton. I always left it fully open when I went down. I stood on top of the hatch as she banged and yelled, and I hammered at the screws in the base of the pottery wheel that Dad had loosened days earlier. It only took a few more smashes and they broke off. Then I dragged it and placed it on top of the hatch. She'd never be able to get out now.

ఌ

The glass door at the back hasn't been fixed. Asha is so lazy; the place looks like a meth-house. Uncle James has left a really annoying note telling me to fix it. He's such a wanker, Uncle James. But I will sort it, course I will. I'm in the courtyard and ahhhh, DD, the wine is working and the paracetamol too. The sun is shining so hard that I could be in Perth. The deckchair Mum found in Meyer's Lane is so comfy and my earphones have cut out all that screaming and banging. I know I've been bad and that I'll be wanting forgiveness soon, but for now, I am going to drink myself into oblivion.

CHAPTER NINETEEN

The Therapist

Jeanie disappeared straight after court on Friday. Off to Mike's probably, or Nigel's, or somewhere as sad. By Monday morning, Joy still hadn't heard from her. Jeanie hadn't answered as many calls from Joy as Joy hadn't answered from Rosie.

Rosie had called almost every hour and left long messages Joy couldn't bring herself to listen to. She would keep ringing till Joy answered, and she loved her for this. But she couldn't pick up yet. She was too busy. By Friday evening she'd arranged a quick sale of the unit to a very friendly man from an efficient equity-release company. She wasn't getting the market price, but that was okay. She was getting more than enough to pay bail, fine, rehab. And she'd be left with plenty to live on – modestly, on the road – for more than enough years. What did she need apart from soup, bread and petrol? She was suddenly desperate to get out of the unit. The smell was really very unpleasant. Inspired by family number nine, she created a Facebook event and spent the weekend in the carport, her furniture and belongings placed neatly in lines, with very reasonable price tags on each item. She was glad to be getting rid of the silver tea set Bertie's mother gave them for their wedding. It was only good for polishing and for show, that thing. Her ornate dressing table needed a sanding and a paint, and for a long time that just reminded her of the energy she no longer had. As for the artwork she thought she would never give up, it reminded her of a period in her life when she had too much time on her hands and too much money. She priced them low. People would probably only be wanting the frames anyway.

She was sad about the mirror, she loved that. It brought in so much light. She might get a hundred dollars for that.

As locals came and went over the weekend, taking kitchen appliances and books and travel mementos and figurines and artwork that once mattered to Joy, she carefully painted the van. She had initially bought white paint, but she nipped to Bunnings to exchange it for lime. If this was her home, it should be the impossible green of England. By the time the Barnards showed up on Sunday she had finished one whole side. It looked fantastic. She also bought a small mattress that Jeanie could sleep on. And she packed Jeanie's special things – like her makeup and her favourite books, as well as Scrabble and cards. She blu-tacked family photos on the cupboard and filled the kitchenette with fun camp food.

'Hello, Joy,' Mrs Barnard said. 'How's it going?'

How did she think it was going?

'Top of the world,' she said. 'Heading off on an adventure.'

'So the mirror's one hundred?' Mr Barnard said. 'There are a few knocks on the frame.'

Joy hadn't haggled once all weekend and was not about to start, not with the Barnards anyway. They had driven two gigantic cars to her garage sale.

'Yes, there are some knocks,' she said.

'The tea set is beautiful,' Mr Barnard said, obviously on behalf of Mrs. What Mr cared about tea sets? 'It's 120?'

'That's too much for us,' said Mrs to Mr; their routine obviously rehearsed. They moved on to look at Joy's jewellery, which was beautifully arranged on her 1890s oak side-table ($50). There were six special pieces in an antique box – presents Bertie had given her on their anniversary: a diamond necklace, an opal ring, a silver bracelet, a pearl necklace, pearl earrings and a gold-and-ruby brooch. Each was priced at $100.

'How much for the lot?' Mr said after Mrs elbowed him.

'Well, they're a hundred each.'

'Six hundred.' Mr had managed the maths.

'Three hundred and it's a deal,' said Mrs.

Joy wished she was the type of person to have the right words ready. She wasn't. She never would be. 'Deal,' she said.

'Or…' Mrs added.

Seriously?

'Add the mirror and the tea set and the dresser and the chest of drawers over there and we'll call it an even five hundred.'

Joy's heart. Her heart. 'Deal,' she said.

She continued painting the van as they loaded their ridiculous vehicles, cursing and swearing at the difficult manoeuvres, obviously wanting Joy to help them. When they eventually drove off, she needed a rest on the dental chair.

Camille was right, that thing was very comfy. She didn't need to remove it. It would do for sleeping, eating and reading.

ఌ

The friendly man was so efficient that the unit in Sebastopol was sold by Monday at lunch time and the money would be hers as soon as the legalities were finalised. She was now a van dweller. Not homeless, not at all. In fact, she had kitted it out with all the essentials, adding lace and embroidered fabric to surfaces that made Joy's heart sing rather than palpitate. She was excited.

She sent emails to her families. She was sorry, but due to health reasons she was retiring. Unhappy families didn't seem to be cheering her up anymore.

She would stay within reach of Jeanie, but she was going

to get into van life. She was going to move about. Her first trip was to Bertolini's café, for a farewell cappuccino.

'Too hot with extra foam,' said Amanda Bertolini.

'One Mrs S coming up,' said Georgio.

She'd only known the Bertolinis a week but she would make sure to come back for coffee. She was planning to tell them this but after taking her first sip she became very dizzy. Instead of driving somewhere beautiful, she parked as close to the hospital as possible and somehow made it to A&E.

∾

Camille was the only person to visit her in the hospital. She had replied so kindly to her retirement message:

I am so sad to hear this, she had written. *You saved me for a while there.*

For a while? Joy replied.

All good, Camille said.

But it didn't sound right. *Are you sure? Where are your mum and dad?*

Camille ignored her question: *What health reasons?*

Just a silly panic attack. I'm in Ballarat Base but they're setting me free soon. I feel a bit of a dill. I'm taking your advice. I'm going to go travelling. I'm going to get into the van life.

You are going to love it! So sorry about the panic, though. Can I help? Would you like me to bring you some decent food?

I need to get out of the house.

Within the hour she arrived with custard tarts and fruit and a decaf cappuccino. She seemed to be drunk. There was something wrong with her hand. Was she limping? She'd either rubbed against the pistil of a lily or had a bruise on her face. 'Are you okay, Camille?'

'I am absolutely positively,' she said. 'Gotta go, Mrs S. Thanks again, and have fun in the van.' She gave Joy a huge hug and a kiss, and staggered out the door.

CHAPTER TWENTY

The Mum

James collected her at 9am, just after the girls yelled goodbye and headed off to court. He was angered by the broken window and the mess, and left a rather shirty message for the girls: *The state of this place! Your poor mother. She's emaciated. I am appalled.*

He left the number of a local glazier and carried Penny to his Range Rover.

The car was smooth and so was the music.

'Wendy's going to feed you up, girly girl. We are going to get you all better.'

She was so sleepy but managed a thank-you.

'That guy,' he said. 'Told you he was bad news from the start. I am not letting you go back to him.'

Penny couldn't handle the usual anti-Andeep rant, which the girls reckoned was as much about his skin colour as his 'non-job'. She stopped the conversation: 'I don't want him back,' she said.

She meant it. She wasn't the type to beg. She did not believe unrequited love was a thing. If one person didn't love the other, then the love did not exist. Anyway, how long since she'd enjoyed any aspect of him, how long since she wanted to have sex with him, since she wanted to hear what he had to say? She would get help, she would get over him. Soon.

'In fact we'd like to shout you to this wellness retreat up north. Wendy's mate swears by it. They recommend a full month. It's for depression, stress, that kind of thing. You're into all that, aren't you?'

It sounded amazing. 'You'd do that?'

'Shit yeah, you're my little sister.'

The Balwyn house and garden had been extended in every direction even though the two boys had their own places in South Yarra now. James's plumbing business was obviously doing very well. Wendy, who had never worked, greeted her like the fifties housewife she was.

'Thank god you're away from that useless cretin,' she said, 'and dear lord, Preston was bad enough, but Ballarat...'

Penny hoped one of the four bedrooms with en-suites had been tidied and set aside for her. She needed to be alone. She needed to be in a bed with the television on. She needed another diazepam and a bottle of wine – there were about seventeen whites in the special, glass wine fridge in the gleaming new kitchen that had no handles anywhere. And there was a stack of red bottles on a quartz shelf above the two coffee makers. This was heaven. Wendy was right. Penny had always lived in dumps.

'Any chance of a drink?' Penny said to Wendy, who had just served her a poached egg on sourdough and a freshly squeezed orange juice.

'Of course.' Wendy eyed the clock and James. They did not approve. They had a plan, and it did not involve wine before lunch.

'Red would be great, just the cheapest.'

'The cheapest, umm,' Wendy said. 'Not sure which one…' She fingered each bottle lovingly, then selected one and handed it to James to open.

'Here you go,' he said. 'You must need this right now.' He poured about an inch into a huge bowl glass then put the bottle on the table about two feet away from her.

'We've set up bedroom number three for you,' Wendy said.

Penny took a sip and let out a sigh of relief. 'Which one is that?'

'Down the corridor, second on the right,' Wendy said.

'I am so thankful. You mind if I have a nap?' She hadn't eaten any of the breakfast.

'Of course, take brekky with you. You need to eat,' said Wendy.

'I will, thank you, I love you, you're life-savers.'

'Oh, and the family chat with Titus and Rudi is at five – they'd love you to join. I'll send you an invite to the family group.'

'What's the wifi?'

'MoloneyKingdom,' Wendy said, 'all one word, cap M cap K.'

Penny took the brekky and the bottle of wine, and headed up the long wide corridor, which was lined with a wall of pristine hardbacks that she'd bet no-one had read. She shut the door and put the food and the wine on the bedside table. Leaflets for The Breathe Retreat were laid out on the bed with the swan-shaped towels. It was in Queensland. The staff wore white linen shirts. There were three pools. There was CBT, anger management, psychoanalysis, hot yoga, reiki, the list went on. Just what she needed.

She opened her laptop, switched on the wifi and messaged the girls:

Hey girls, hope court went okay and that you're both getting some space now. It's been such a difficult time and I am really sorry for what's been happening with me and your dad. It will be a huge relief for you to get home, Asha, back to work. James left a glazier's number to fix the door – can you see to this, Cam? I'm at James's. Feeling a bit better, but I won't be here long. James and Wendy are shouting me a four-week residential in Queensland to sort my issues – I know I have so many! Your dad and I will both always love you. And we will do our best to be better parents; maybe it'll be easier to do when we're not having to try so hard to be happy together. Please look after each other. Mum x

She opened Andeep's Facebook page. She'd changed his password after he left but hadn't done anything crazy, thankfully. Even now, she stopped herself from making comments.

She texted his mobile:

Hi, sending you the photos we chose at Hall's Gap.

She attached the pictures to her text – of the wedding parties in Glasgow and Melbourne, summers in Portsea.

I don't want to make you feel guilty. Neither of us should feel bad about the end of us. We did well, for a really long time. We have two amazing girls. PS, I changed your Facebook password after you left, sorry, it's Fuck1ngPr1ck! Penny

CHAPTER TWENTY-ONE

The Second Born

FRIDAY: After closing the hatch, I wiped myself out drinking and snoozing in the sun until a message woke me – Mum. I shocked myself with the perfection and succinctness of my reply, which was this:

Fuck you.

I don't regret it. I don't have anything to add. How many times have I asked for help since Asha moved home? *She broke my fucking nose! We need family therapy! I need help!* All she did was tut-tut us both – 'Oh you *two*!' – or tell me off for needling her and being whiney. It was better when we were little, but when I think about it she never stood up for me then either. She was just around more. And I was so in awe of Asha I didn't question her stardom; her status as the best, the cleverest, the one who knows, the one who is always right, the one who must be obeyed.

Dad helped when I was younger. We'd do things together, and he'd make me feel safe and important. He'd read to me at night for ages: everything from Katie Morag to Robbie Burns. He'd take me to the theatre to see things Asha and Mum weren't into, like *The Lion King* and *Les Mis* and stand-up shows for children, which we both decided were patronising and unfunny. When I was a bit older we got into zombie shows, and he'd scratch my back softly on the sofa as we watched heads being shot and stabbed and stomped on. Fuck him too. Where is he now?

I think I might hate my mother. I think I might hate my father. It's making me feel better, writing that down. I hate my parents. Get them both to fuck. I'm sleepy again, seeya later.

ↄ৴

I just put my ear against the floor, just next to the pottery wheel. Asha was praying, not to Nellie – not sure she wants that kid to come back to life anymore – just to Gee-suss etc.

'Asha?' I said.

She stopped praying.

'If I open it will you stop beating me up?'

I could hear her climbing the ladder.

'You have to promise or I won't open it.'

She was at the top. I could hear her.

'Do you promise?'

Nothing. She was pushing at the hatch. I sat on the pottery wheel.

'Do you promise?' She was taking so long to answer that

I did a twirl on the wheel. I was aware, doing this, that I might be going slightly mad.

'Yes,' she said, with a bad voice.

'Really really?' I said, still twirling.

'Really really.' Good voice this time but I could tell she was finding it hard to pull off.

I dragged the wheel away from the hatch and prised the stone open about an inch with the screwdriver. Asha's evil cat-eyes glinted at me through the crack and startled me. I opened it another centimetre and could see that her face was not the kind to keep promises. She pushed against the stone with all her might, growling, 'You fucking arsehole! I AM GOING TO KILL YOU!'

Before I knew it I had tossed the screwdriver and jumped on the bluestone, slamming it back into position. I could hear a bang and a scream. She had fallen from the ladder.

Silence. Oh dear, I'd hurt her.

'LET ME OUT, LET ME OUT YOU FUCKING BITCH!'

No, the fall hadn't changed her a bit. She was the same old Asha as she ever was. I dragged the pottery wheel back in place and shut the bedroom door.

The glazier came in the evening and fixed the back door. I let him in the back gate and closed off the hall, so he couldn't hear a thing. I fell asleep in the mezzanine with the screwdriver under my pillow.

ↄ

SATURDAY: By this afternoon Asha had stopped yelling and banging, and I just couldn't get enough of the peace and quiet. I pottered round, tidying things up. The house is cosy now. I'm liking it. Fatima from uni phoned, and I told her I'm going to Perth and will be in touch when I get back, but I am never gonna ring her back. What kind of best friend is she anyway? She hasn't visited me once since I moved here. I've visited her three times. It's like Ballarat's in South America or something. I've moved myself into the mezzanine. I've filled thirty black rubbish bags with Dad's stuff and fourteen with all the broken rubbish Mum's never going to upcycle. The bike shed is stuffed full.

ↄ

SUNDAY: Thirty-one degrees today! Spock rang and I told him I'm not wanting to see him anymore. I reckon he's just hoping I've tried the stuff in the tin and that I'll want to pay for it now, that's the way they do it, I've heard. I read two books in the courtyard. I'm a bit burnt.

ↄ

MONDAY: The guy from the lolly shop at Sovereign Hill rang saying there's a shift available two weeks on Monday. I told him I wasn't looking for work anymore because I had won the lottery. Asha yelled this morning so she's okay but still scary. She'll be safe down there unless she falls down the shaft. There's plenty of biccies and wine, candles too, and two blankies. I reckon she's just taking turns at drinking and sleeping and praying.

&

Later: Fuckety fuck, she's not made any noise for yonks, and she's defo not on the ladder and I'm panicking that the tagging people will notice non-movement. Maybe the alarm will beep if she stays still for too long. I've Googled it and I can't find any info, but I reckon they'd check for dead offenders, don't ya think? The cops might show up at the door. Or the mental-health people for that court assessment. Or the alcohol counsellor she's supposed to see. Shite, I am really going to have to open that thing up and let her out. I know what I'll do. I'll open it before I go out. It's not like she'll tell the cops or the psychs or the counsellor that it's terrible here and she wants to leave. They'll send her to jail if she says that. I have all the power for once. It feels good.

&

Dad's big event tonight. I'm going. Gonna pop in and see Mrs S first.

I've just written a note for Asha:

Sorry, but I was scared what you might do to me. Truce?

Gonna just move the wheel and leave the note on top of it and open that hatch fast as I can and make a run for it.

Wish me luck!

CHAPTER TWENTY-TWO

The Second-Born

I've changed since I watched Dad's video the other day. I thought he was funny then. I was happy he'd made his escape; I hadn't taken it in that his escape was also from me.

There was a huge crowd at the Eureka – crazy numbers, DD, like more than half full, and it's humungous. Never been there before but I was in awe when I took my seat. Felt like London probably is – ornate ceiling and carved wood and tons of velvet. He'd always gone on about the gigs he did in the old days, but I never listened properly. It was all so ancient. I had a seat twenty rows from the front, and when he came on I had this burst of love that brought tears to my eyes, made my jaw tingle. Pride, I guess. The crowd had been warmed up by some dude from Wagga Wagga, so when he came on everyone was heavily clappy and up for a laugh. Me too, which surprised me, cos I'd gone expecting to heckle him. I even took one of the eggs Asha didn't throw at me the other day in case he said something really annoying and he needed an egg thrown at him. On the way there I practised some lines I could yell, none of which were very clever: 'Fuck You and Fuck Off.' Stuff like that. Very disappointing, my heckling ideas. When the usher directed me to my seat I realised I'd never manage to throw the egg that far, and it cracked in my pocket when I took my seat anyway. I was so hot that it had cooked on my leg about ten minutes later.

The jaw-tingling pride transformed into something quite different as he dissected his terrible marriage to my mother. Embarrassment, I suppose. Till a month ago I always thought of them as a great couple, doing creative things together, making new plans, not afraid to live differently from wankers like Uncle James and most of the rest of the world. I tried to make myself smaller, slipping down into my stinking, scrambled-egg seat, hoping no-one would recognise me. My head started buzzing, like I had tinnitus or something, and I could hardly make out what he was saying. But I knew he'd moved on to talk about his kids. Something about the parents always being blamed and how unfair that is. Something about the dream of the empty nest. Something about he and Mum having to run away from home. And the kids, those little fuckers – *grown adults* – following, sponging, sucking the life out of them. I was so fried-eggy that the people next to me moved to the back halfway through. If they gave me dirty looks I didn't notice cos I was concentrating on my feet, hoping to be as small as them; that if I used the power of my mind hard enough I might fit into my shoes. I wondered about the power of prayer – if I did it with gusto like Asha I might be able to disappear. Please god, turn me into nothing, make me invisible, oh lord, turn me into air.

A lot of clapping. A standing ovation. A Vanessa at the side of the stage, hugging him, holding his hand and leading him backstage.

Everyone was leaving the usual way, out the front. I made my way backstage. I don't know what I wanted to say to him. Not fuck you or get fucked, something else. Help, maybe. Come help me, Dad. Make me safe. Make me important. I raced down corridors, out the back door. But I was too late. He and Vanessa were driving off.

'Dad!' I yelled.

One of the security guys looked at me with a smile. 'He's your dad?'

'Yes. Is there an after party or something? Do you know where they're going?'

'The Big Smoke. He's doing another performance at The Comedy Lounge in two hours. He's booked solid for weeks, off to the UK soon. You must be very proud.'

'I must be,' I said.

He looked at me more closely and sniffed. 'Is that egg?'

'Yeah, sorry,' I said. I cried all the way home.

☙

Omg she's not come out. I've locked myself in the bathroom to write this, just in case, but when I crept down the ladder into the hole she was lying on a blanket and snoring. I've left the hatch open still so she can come out when she wants. But maybe she likes it down there. I did. There's still some wine, after all, and that's all she wants and cares about now The Dick is out of her life. I put a pillow under her head, another blankie on top, a bottle of water beside her. I was so scared climbing back up, thought she might grab my ankle and yank me down, but she didn't wake.

It's cooling down at last, it's dark. I'm exhausted. What a week.

Gonna have a rest now, so it's night night. Is it weird to say I love you to a diary? I do, though. I love you, DD. Please keep me safe, please help me, please look after me, I love you. Amen.

CHAPTER TWENTY-THREE

The Therapist

Joy was finding it difficult to be positive about van life. Even the embroidered doilies her grandmother gifted for her 'glory box' didn't lift her spirits much, especially after she spilled tea all over the daffodil one, which was her favourite. She really needed to go to the toilet. There was a contraption in the cupboard that she'd looked at several times. Portapotty, it was called. Bertie had probably used it when he was on the road for those few months before he went bust. He'd left the instruction leaflet on top, and Joy had read it three times. She could do this, surely. But every time she read it she couldn't help but focus on the cleaning process – and how to avoid splashback. She had to face facts – she was not going to risk a Portapotty splashback. She was not a country girl, she was not a happy camper.

She exited the hospital on Monday as the sun was setting, holding her heavy handbag and a paper bag containing Valium and beta blockers. The van was parked one block away, in the MacDonald's carpark. The short walk exhausted her, and she was surprised when she saw the van – the side with the huge white mouth was facing her and the smile was crazy-sinister. She hadn't managed to paint both sides lime green yet – and when she saw the other side, she wondered if it was a good idea anyway. It was ugly, not the green of England at all. She decided it was the worst-looking vehicle in the vicinity. A shock, as she'd selected this carpark carefully.

She sat in the driver's seat and tried Jeanie's number several more times. Still no answer. She really needed to go to the loo. She didn't want to use the Macdonald's facilities as she'd need to purchase something and that would mess with her already-strained digestive system. Where could she park for the night? She'd never researched van life as she had never yearned to travel, not since finding herself in love on the other side of the earth from everything she cared about. Since then she had only ever yearned to go home, just like in that on-repeat song of hers, 'Wayfaring Stranger'. She had always wanted to go home to see her mother (dead), to see her father (dead) to see her sister (oh, to see her sister). She did not want to roam. Bertie took her camping once when they were courting, and she didn't sleep a wink, ended up with a sore back and constipation that took several days to sort. The idea of heading off any which way until somewhere beautiful beckoned made her take one of the beta blockers and one of the Valium.

Dear oh dear. She should have read the side-effects. She probably shouldn't drive after taking the Valium. She decided to wait a couple of hours, perhaps have a rest in the dental chair, then Google camp sites. She would pay for a place with power and a loo and a shower. She might even make some friends there.

She made herself a cup of tea and zuzzed the dental chair till it was horizontal. Eye patches on, Joy started to feel much better.

'Scuse me!'

Joy woke to banging. It took her a while to realise where she was. In a dental van in a MacDonald's carpark. A male police officer was knocking on the front door, peering in the window. She was glad she'd covered her legs with a blankie. She buzzed the chair upright and crawled through to the driver's seat to wind down the window.

'Hello, officer.'

'You're sleeping here?'

'I was napping. I'd just…' She was about to tell him about hospital and Valium then thought better of it. Good gracious, she had done something wrong already. Van life was tricky. 'I was just going to look for a camp site, actually. Sorry, I'll be on my way.'

'Napping eh?'

'Only for a…' Actually Joy didn't know how long she'd slept. Longer than she realised, the sun was setting. 'Not for long. Sorry, it won't happen again.'

'No it won't,' he said. He banged her door so hard it made

her jump. 'Now move on, Mrs, don't let me see you here again.'

She moved on.

So this was what it was like to be a criminal. This was what it was like to be homeless. Not that she was either one of these things, not at all. This was not good for her heart.

She found herself driving to that Mike person's house outside town. She parked behind a tree, hoping to spot Jeanie, or hoping not to. She wasn't sure which. Loud music was playing from the ramshackle brick house. One of the front windows was broken. More car parts and an armchair had arrived on the grass since she'd last visited, and four poor-quality vehicles were parked in the driveway. She couldn't see through the broken windows, but she imagined Jeanie lying on a soiled sofa in there, or sitting on the bare floor smoking a pipe with her eyes rolling round, or dancing wildly on a table while talking fast about great ideas. She'd seen enough over the last two years to know what that stuff does to people. About a year ago, she found Jeanie climbing the walls, literally. Or trying to. And on another occasion, after two day's driving around, looking for her daughter, Joy answered the phone to this:

'Mum, mum mum mum, I'm with Dad. I'm with Dad. He's here. He's pouring you a sweet sherry. You'll never believe it, he's got a beard! I'm going to put him on now. He's desperate to talk to you.'

Joy hung up. She did not like meth talk. She did some Googling after that. Her daughter was obviously delusional; experiencing some kind of psychotic episode. Reality and Ice were adversaries. And Mike's house was not good for her heart. She heard a woman yelling inside, something smashing, then loud laughter. Some bail address.

She drove to St Pat's. She'd been so busy packing and selling on the weekend that she had missed Mass – and confession – for the first time in years. She had so much to confess. The church was open, but there was no-one around. A sense of hopelessness was taking hold and she must not let it happen. Hope was up there with faith and family – they were Joy's strongholds. Parked outside the gothic church, she wondered about all those positive quotes about families that she spouted off all the time in her sessions – the kind of sayings Father Nigel congratulated her for believing and upholding: that family is the most important thing in the world; that it is but an earlier heaven; that it's one of nature's masterpieces.

She had missed her weekly visit to Bertie's grave, too, so made that her next stop. It was dark by the time she parked at the gate and she was too scared to go in. Anyway, what was the point visiting graves? What was the point talking to a piece of ground? What was the point in anything? That hopelessness, she really must banish it.

She looked at the Portapotty leaflet then drove as fast as

she could to the unit in Sebastopol. She'd spend the night in the carport. The unit might be sold already, but no-one would have moved in yet. She still had the keys. At least she could use the loo.

After her ablutions, Joy heated baked beans on the small cooker in the van, hoping the experience would excite her as it had Camille. Alas, it was all very depressing really. She thought about crying. When Rosie rang again, she answered, surprised that as her words came out, so did tears.

'Hello,' she said.

'Oh my god, thank god. Turn on your video,' Rosie said.

'I don't want you to see me.'

'Turn it on, you know the button. Where are you?'

'In the van.'

'I need to see you. Take a seat, put the phone somewhere stable in front of you, turn on video.'

She did as she was told. It took ages. When she saw her sister's face, she wanted to cry more than ever.

'Blossy,' Rosie said, 'look at you! I'm so sorry about Jeanie. Thank you for answering. Don't hang up, please, stay on.' Rosie was tearful too. She was sitting on her sofa in the cottage. Joy could see out the window into her garden. She could see the barn out back, a renovation project Rosie had lost interest in. There was snow on the roof.

'There's snow!' she said. 'I love snow.'

'Snow loves you,' Rosie said.

'Does snow? Does snow love me?' Joy was sobbing like a five-year-old.

Rosie was reacting like a three-year-old. 'Almost as much as I do. If you blow your nose I'll love you more.'

Joy laughed, reached for an ironed hankie, had a good blow. 'I'm starting to wonder if families are a good thing. All those things I say to clients about families being blah blah blah – all my clients hate each other, they all tear each other apart. And my daughter, my own little girl.'

'She's forty-three.'

'She's my baby.'

'She's peri-menopausal.'

'She's my wee Jeanie and she has no-one else.'

'You look pale. Are you okay?'

'I was in hospital today.'

'Oh god, why?'

'Silly old panic attack, thought I was going to die. But I didn't,' she said with regret.

'You've got to chuck her,' Rosie said.

'What, chuck who?'

'Jeanie. You've got to chuck her. Leave her. Dump her. Drop her. Get the hell away from there. Come to me. Come here now, tonight, tomorrow morning, get on a flight and live here. George is away all the time. I am bored out of my brain. You've got cash from the sale of the unit, bring that and stay here with me.'

'You are joking?'

'This is how it is – are you listening to me? Actually I would love it if you wrote this down.'

'I don't have a pen.'

'Your daughter is killing herself with that stuff. It's almost inevitable that she will die. If she gets through it, by some miracle, it will not be because you saved her. And if you keep trying, if you keep living your life for her you will die as well. Soon, by the looks. Is that bad foundation or are you orange?'

'I'm orange.'

'There are two options,' she said. 'One, you die trying to save her.'

Joy was hating Rosie's rant, she was also loving it.

'Or, *two*: you live. Here. With me. You can love her from over here. Leave some money at the rehab for one more shot. You can ring her, Skype, all the things we've done to keep close. We've been loving each other for fifty years, have we not? We've managed. I still know you, you still know me. We've looked after each other from afar.'

'But you've got George and the kids and the grandkids. I'm Jeanie's only family. What about blood being thicker than water?'

'It is not thicker than Ice,' said Rosie.

CHAPTER TWENTY-FOUR

The Second-Born

I think the meth is really helping. It's hard to write fast enough, but I'm going to try because I need to get my thoughts in order. I'm going to have another go soon but I need a rest. I scrubbed and cleaned forever, including and especially my bedroom, but mostly I've been trying so so hard. My hands are shaky, sorry about the writing. It's been twenty-four hours since it happened and it's still not working. But I can't give up. I won't. I just need to try harder. I need to get my thoughts straight. I need to focus.

It started on Monday after I got back from Dad's gig. The hatch was open like I left it and Asha was still asleep in the cellar. I went to bed in the mezzanine and I was dreaming that Asha was putting toothpaste in my thingy jing. Eight years old, telly on, sofa. She was straddling me, pinning me down, her legs were on my arms. My party dress, she was lifting it up. I couldn't see my tummy cos the red checked material was all gathered and bunched under my neck. I kicked and kicked. I tried to jab my knees into her back. I tried to lift my head and bang it into her but it wouldn't reach. Nothing would make her stop.

I was a wriggling upside-down insect, and she was laughing like a witch. I tried to free my arms from under her legs but they wouldn't budge. I tried to move my torso from side to side, see if that would set me free so I could reach down and flick her hand away from you-know-what, but I couldn't. *Get away*, I was trying to say in my dream, but nothing came out. *Get off. Help*: nothing. I couldn't breathe. I could feel scraping, scratching, oozing, filling, tugging, stretching.

I woke up.

Tug-tug. Something *was* happening down there, an ungodly stretching.

TUG – something yanked at it so hard it hurt.

I turned the light on and there she was. Asha, about five feet away from me, standing, staring, a smirk on her face, one hand by her side, the other weirdly animated and holding something round and plastic.

She moved her hand as if sewing or conducting an orchestra, and I felt it again and then looked down and saw. My *you know what* was stretching in sync with her hand movements.

There was a small knot in the gold hoop of the ring she gave me for my twenty-first birthday; the fishing wire mum uses to cut clay and make jewellery. It was almost invisible but was becoming clearer as I followed the knot from my pus-filled piercing across the room to Asha, who was holding the other end on its plastic reel. She smiled, raised her eyebrow and made a small pulling movement again.

'Time to get up,' she said, taking a step backward, jerking my grossly oversized thing harder than before, forcing me to jump from the bed and lurch forward to grab the wire.

I couldn't get hold of it. She moved her arm up and down, side to side. It was impossible to see. 'Stop, stop,' I said, finally managing to grab it. But my hand, like the rest of me, was wet with sweat and I couldn't get a purchase. It kept slipping through my fingers, and Asha kept moving it.

'Asha, please forgive me. I was just scared. I won't do it again.'

'What is it with you and your belly button?' she said. 'Is it because you don't like where you came from? It's so funny.' She took another step backward.

I stumbled forward and grabbed the wire with my wet hand. I was trying to twirl it round my wrist when she moved back again, jerking me forward. I wondered about throwing something at her. The bedside lamp, maybe I could grab that really fast and hurl it at her. But she was jerking me forward with tiny little yanks like I was a cod, and I kept dry heaving.

'Jesus wouldn't want this,' I said. 'Hail Mary full of grace. Our Father who art in heaven.' I wished I knew at least one full prayer.

'Too late, Camille, you are going to hell.' She took

another huge step backward and yanked me forward. 'In fact, I am going to take you there now.'

It was on. She was running and so was I. Across the mezzanine and down the stairs, two at a time. I was screaming, crying, trying not to fall: 'Stop, please, stop, it hurts. Stop!'

The wire between her hand and my stomach area maintained its tension the whole way down to the kitchen. I had no time to grab, no time to press a hand against the thing to stop an inevitable tearing, there was only running. Keep up, Cam, just keep up. My feet were bare and slippy. She had runners on; had planned this to a tee and was so fast, so fit. I couldn't gain on her to loosen the tension, I was always five feet behind, the wire a tight, straight line between us – the thing stretched out at least an inch from where it was. I was the water-skier and she was the boat. I managed to keep up with her through the kitchen, into the huge hall and into my bedroom. As she entered, she grabbed an axe. She must have got it from the courtyard and planted it there – she was ever the planner, our Asha, so thorough and hard-working. She pointed the axe at me as she moved backward into the corner of the room. She had done the maths: her arms + axe = five feet. The wire remained taut therefore, the blade of the axe almost touching my face.

'Get in the hole,' she said.

I was a few feet from it and she had very little space to

manoeuvre. To get me in, she'd need cooperation and a lot of fear.

'No,' I said.

'Get in the hole,' she said again, jabbing my chin with the blade of the axe.

'I will not.' I made a move forward, axe blade now at my neck. 'What are you going to do, are you going to chop me up?'

'Maybe,' she said, 'if you don't get in the hole.'

I swiped at the wooden handle of the axe with my hand, and she almost lost hold of it but sadly didn't. As I lunged forward, hoping to restrain her, she smashed the blunt side of the blade across my knees, and I fell flat on the bluestone floor, stomach first.

By the time I got over the pain and lifted my chin, she had moved backward to the doorway and now had the space to shepherd me. She started dragging me, inch by inch, towards the hole. Splayed out on my tummy, I put my hand underneath me to cover the piercing and stop it from scraping across the stone. Another inch.

'Get in the hole,' she said.

Another inch. She was sheepdogging me, rounding me up.

My head was hovering across the opening to the cellar. I stretched my arm out to stop myself from falling in, head first. Another inch, another. My shoulders had reached the hatch. My stomach now. I was lying across it.

She put her foot on my back. She had an axe in her hand. She had wire tied to my belly button and was shortening it, winding it back onto the reel. It was four feet, three feet, two and a half feet from my belly button. I'm gonna write those words from now on. Belly button. Belly button. I can now because of what I did next.

I closed my eyes and counted to myself. *One … two …* I could do this I could do this. And … *three*.

I ripped it out. Just like that. Must've been anger, I didn't feel a thing. And now I don't have a belly button. Ha. I don't have a belly button belly button belly button belly button.

I didn't move after the rippage, I just lay there, still as I could, as if nothing had happened at all. Heroic, me reckons. A master at playing dead. Torso covering the hatch, I rubbed my hand on my T-shirt and held the wire as tightly as I could so she didn't know what I'd just done. She couldn't see a thing, didn't have a clue there was blood pouring out of me and into the cellar. She still had her foot on my back. She was still holding her fishing wire. She thought she had won.

'Okay, okay,' I said, 'I'll get in. But not head first. Let me sit up.'

She didn't move her foot off my back.

'Please, Asha.' I used my vulnerable voice, and after a second or two she took her foot off. I could hear her releasing some more wire and stepping back a bit.

My mind was racing almost as much as it is now. How do I do this, how do I do this? Then it came to me. Hand covering my belly, I took my time to lift myself into a kneeling position on the other side of the hatch from Asha, then, fast as a whip, twirled the wire round my arm and pulled as hard as I could.

It didn't do what I wanted. She didn't have a strong enough hold on the reel to be catapulted forward and fall down the stairs. But it did surprise her enough to drop the axe and lose concentration. I stood up and roared. My hands outstretched, ready to strangle or batter or shake or all of the above, and with blood spewing from the place where my belly button used to be, I hurtled towards her and pushed her chest as hard as I could.

Must have been a decent push, I think the roaring gave me superhuman strength. I see it in slow motion now, her falling back, the reel dropping from her hand, flying through the air, her face scared at last, her hands flailing, unable to save her from smashing against the wall and ricocheting down to the floor, her head hitting the edge of the pottery wheel.

I honestly thought I'd killed her. She stopped moving immediately. Her eyes stayed open. Her expression didn't change: terrified, surprised.

'Asha?' I said.

Nothing changed. Eyes still open.

'Asha?' I shook her shoulders gently. 'Asha? Wake up, wake

up.' I slapped her face, I breathed into her mouth. 'Please, please Asha, say something, speak, speak to me.'

I did CPR for ages. I breathed into her mouth over and over. I kissed her cheek and I told her I loved her, and I begged and I even prayed: 'Dear god, dear god please don't let her die. Wake up Asha, please.'

I was about to get my phone and call 000 and it happened. She took in a huge crackle of air. The effort and shock made her sit up as she did it.

She woke up. She totally woke, DD. Can you believe it? Writing about it now I am smiling my head off because it did happen. Twenty-five hours ago, but it defo happened. And I was hardly even trying then.

'Thank god, thank god,' I said to her, kissing her cheek again, hugging her tight. 'I'm so sorry, Asha.'

'What are you doing to me?' That's what she said with that lovely deep voice of hers.

I hugged her. 'You're alive, thank god.' I was incredulous. 'I thought you were dead.' Seriously, she hadn't moved or blinked for ages. And yet here she was, sitting up, right as rain. I wasn't thinking about miracles and Nellie and all that, I was just so happy she was alive.

'Can we stop this fighting?' I said. 'You're my big sister. I love you. Can you forgive me?'

She stared ahead for yonks, then eventually looked at me and said: 'Forgive you for what?'

It was her angry face now. She would wait for my response. She had plenty of time.

I realised there were a lot of things I needed to be forgiven for, a whole list. If I got it wrong, if I missed anything, I would not be forgiven, this would not be over.

'I'm sorry for pushing you just now, for locking you in the cellar.' I was already finding it so difficult not to add a 'but'.

'Uh-huh,' she said, sitting up, straightening her back against the wall, cracking her neck.

'I'm sorry I didn't tell you about Richard and Rowena. I should have told you I saw them. They made me promise and I didn't know what to do. I was really confused.'

'Uh-huh,' she said, pulling herself to a standing position and hovering above me.

I followed suit and stood up. It hurt my stomach so much that I doubled over for a second.

Asha had her hands on her hips. She stared, didn't move. She was waiting for the rest of my apologies. Far as I could see, she didn't have a single injury. And yet here I was with a crooked nose, a buttonless, bleeding belly and bruises all over me.

I should have just kept going. I should have said sorry about the thoughtless T-shirt I got her from Victoria market and sorry for not calling her more often and sorry for getting on better with Dad and sorry for not caring enough about Mum and sorry for ruining the toothpaste and sorry that

Wes flirted with me at the barbecue that time and sorry for accidentally being better than her at one or two things, but I didn't.

Probs good, I wouldn't have sounded very sorry. Truth is, I was all out of apologies.

'Truce?' I said, holding out my bloody and aching hand.

But she didn't shake it, she turned and walked out into the hall.

I slid down against the wall and replaced my blood-soaked T-shirt with a fresh one. I was wondering about an ambulance. I needed to ring 000. She'd banged her head, she might have a concussion. But if I did that she'd get in trouble. She'd go to jail. So I got up to go see how she was.

Before I made it to the door she was coming at me. She had something in her hand, couldn't tell what it was then, but I know now cos she stabbed my shoulder with it and I had to pull it out a while later. It was that blunt clay-sculpting tool she threatened to kill herself with at the open house. Not so blunt, turns out. What was I sposed to do, let her kill me? She'd stabbed me ffs. And she wasn't stopping there. She had me by the hair, clumps of it came out. I'm gonna have to shave my head I reckon, DD. There are patches. Lucky I've got a decent-shaped head.

It hurt so much, made me really angry. I think I might have punched her in the nose a few times, quite a few. I shouldn't have done that. She wound up on the ground.

I shouldn't have kicked her while she was down either ... and kicked her again – I am so bad. And kicked her and kicked her and shoved her with my feet and my hands till she toppled down the stairs and landed with a thud on the cellar floor. Wish I could take all that back. I really am sorry for that.

༄

DD, I still can't wake her up, she won't wake up. It's Wednesday morning, she hasn't moved at all for twenty-five hours. I'm so worried about the ankle bracelet. If she keeps not moving, the police will show up. I just know they will. I tried to carry her up the stairs a few hours ago. Put her on my back. Only made it a few steps before she fell off. I think I made things worse. I should try again maybe, do you think?

Her eyes have been shut the whole time. She won't open them and there's a weirdness about the shape of her. She's all skewwhiff. I had to use bicarb of soda to get blood off the floors. It took so, so long. I've done three loads of washing and I've scrubbed the whole house over and over. I don't know whether I should straighten her leg or not. I can see her knee bone and what looks like mashed potato inside. Think her leg snapped at the knee with the first fall, almost came off second time round. It's disgusting. I've been throwing up tons and have had to clean that up too. There's nothing left in me. I should eat something. I need to keep trying. I need to move her too. If I don't we're both fucked.

Hang on, what was that?

Thought I heard her breathe but no.

Back in a minute, I need to focus, just going to have another tiny little puff of the stuff in Spock's tin.

℃

The answers just come at you! I fixed a HUGE problem; brought the axe back down with me and did the count to three thing – I can do this, I can do this – one, two ... and three. I had two good swings at the knee-bone and cut it right off, which is great because I can just move the ankle bracelet round the house now and the electronic people won't suspect a thing. I couldn't slide the tag off unfortunately. Asha has such hefty calves, poor thing. It's in the bath at the moment. I took it upstairs in a bucket and it was nearly full by the time I got there. Gross. I left the tap on and I think the blood will be gone by now. I am breathing easy at last, phew. The tagging folk won't be ringing the bell anytime soon. I can focus on waking her up now, put all my energy into it.

If I stroke her face at least fifty times it gets warm but I have to do it quite firmly with both hands and from top to bottom top to bottom. I'm finding that if I chant at the same time – 'Rise, Asha, Rise, I want to see your beautiful smile, I want to look into your beautiful eyes' – it gets warm, the life comes back a bit. I've played some of the music R and R and Asha and the others on those RTD sites sing too – songs about Jesus and Lazarus and healing and stuff – but I don't think the music is making a difference yet. Worth a try, though. I'm not going to give up.

Back in a sec, just gonna rub her face and chant for another fifty then move her tag etc to the lounge. They might get suspicious if she's in the bath too long.

CHAPTER TWENTY-FIVE

The Therapist

Joy headed for St Pat's on Tuesday afternoon, where she confessed to a desperate desire to jump on a plane. Father Nigel gave her five Our Fathers and five Hail Marys and she was annoyed when she left. He should have spoken sternly to her like Father Tom back in Winchester did at her very first confession. She was eight years old and did not take the advice of her kindly teacher – 'just say you hit your brother or your sister'. Instead she said, 'I stole a shilling from the collection plate last week.' She really wanted to get it off her chest. It had been eating her up ever since.

Father Tom had growled at eight-year-old Joy: 'You did what!?' He lectured her very loudly for at least five minutes, with all her friends waiting their turn outside, and made her do an entire rosary.

What did priests know about family loyalty, she decided, as she made her way from St Pat's to the van. She couldn't think of anything more despicable than abandoning a daughter in need, no matter how old Jeanie was; no matter how kind and convincing her sister was. She would not do it. There, that was it, she had made up her mind. She would never leave Jeanie. Five Our Fathers and five Hail Marys. An insult to family. She completed a rosary, phoned the rehabilitation unit and paid for another three months. They were very understanding and agreed to hold the money for when Jeanie was ready.

She then drove off in search of her daughter, this time hitting the jackpot immediately. She was in The Old Smithy, the meth corner, with five people who were drooly and dangerous-looking, their ages spanning at least thirty years. Joy was terrified to approach the group. She took a seat at a table on the other side of the bar. It seemed a long time before she caught Jeanie's eye and smiled.

Jeanie smiled back and waved but didn't come over.

Joy gestured – come to me.

Jeanie began talking at a hundred miles an hour to a twenty-something girl, who talked back faster. Jeanie rolled her eyes. The girl laughed and looked at Joy. She was highly intoxicated, or under the influence, or whatever they call it when it's methamphetamine. Joy should be empathetic, perhaps she should try and help. If the young woman wasn't looking over and guffawing like an absolute bully, she might have.

They were obviously talking about her. Even as a hormonal adolescent, Jeanie hadn't treated her with such contempt. It was sad that Joy was accustomed to it now. Since Bertie's death, disrespect had been the norm. Mother-daughter montage scenes were few and far between. Joy couldn't smile when she gestured the second time. Her face was very hot, and she was losing the sensation in her legs. The chairs at this grotty old pub were made for fitter people.

Eventually, Jeanie put her drink down and came over. 'Hi Mum,' she said flatly and without affection.

'Hey, darling, are you okay?'

Jeanie was skin and bone and not into the hug. 'Yeah, I'm great. How are you?'

'I'm good. I'm good. I'm worried about you.'

'Excellent, mind if I get back? Just in the middle of a really interesting conversation.'

Joy took her daughter's hand. 'Jeanie, come home, please come home with me. Well it's the van now, I sold the unit.'

She laughed. 'You're living in the van?'

Joy was a bit hurt that she didn't care about the unit, but didn't say anything. 'It's very comfy. There's a mattress for you. I washed and ironed your favourite linen.'

'Thanks, Mum, but Mike's putting me up. It's my bail address so I can't anyway. Let's meet up later in the week though, yeah?'

The motley crew had moved out into the beer garden to smoke. Jeanie seemed desperate to follow them. Perched on the edge of the chair she kept crooking her neck, legs fidgeting, poised to pounce, desperate to get away from her mortifying, daggy old bag of a mother.

'Please, Jeanie. At least come and see the van, it's just parked outside. We'd be cosy as could be.'

'And what would we do, Mum, play board games?' Jeanie was looking at the door to the beer garden. 'Fuck's sake, maybe you don't have a life, but I do.'

Horrid Jeanie was back in all her glory. Joy's heart started going. She needed her medication. 'I've paid for another go at rehab, for when you're ready. You just have to show up.'

'Thanks, Mum,' she said. 'Can we talk later, Friday maybe?'

'Just come and take a look at the van, please at least come and look at it.'

'Okay, okay, I will. I'll just go tell my friends. Back in a sec.' She headed out the back door.

That lovely boy who served the chewy steak was working again. 'Nothing for me tonight thanks, Gregory,' she said, despite the fact that he hadn't asked, 'just waiting for my daughter. How are you doing today, busy?'

'No worries,' he said, not hearing what she said, and taking a tray of pots to the alcoholics' table. She was getting a tad tired of not being heard by the likes of lovely Gregory.

Five minutes later and Jeanie still hadn't come back inside. Joy made her way to the beer garden, nervous. She was very intimidated by the group, most of all by her own daughter. Jeanie would probably say something mean in front of everyone and make her feel even tinier than she was – she must have lost half a stone in the last two weeks; moving home twice had taken its toll. They would probably all laugh at her. She wondered what it was they could possibly find funny; what would Jeanie say to make them laugh at her?

Check out her lipstick.

I grew up in Downton Abbey.

She lives in a dental van.

Joy opened the back door and peered outside. There was no-one in the beer garden. Jeanie and her anti-social bully-crew had done a runner.

જ

Joy parked in a campsite out of town that night. She didn't enjoy the tinned soup she heated. The communal area was not much chop either. There were three happy families in it: one at the pool table; one making pancakes; one playing Monopoly. She had a go at patience three times but didn't manage to get it out. No-one talked to her or even smiled. Perhaps she would never make any friends in this new van life of hers. Before getting into bed, if a dental chair could be called a bed, she donned her slippers and crossed camp to the bathroom. It was mostly very clean except that someone had deposited at least one hundred dark pieces of snot all over the toilet wall. Some kind of protest, or mental-health issue, by the looks. She forgot to take her toothbrush and her conditioner, and she needed to buy a warmer dressing gown. After making her chair up with a flat sheet and a single quilt and exactly the wrong pillows, she messaged Jeanie again. No response. She zuzzed the chair as horizontal as it would go and closed her eyes for about two seconds before a voice scared the living daylights out of her. A man speaking sternly, a child whining: just a family walking past. She would have to get used to that. She zuzzed the chair upright and got up to check the cabinet filled with dental equipment. She should probably have some sort of protection with her at night. But what? The drill, the plaque remover? No, the scalpel. She put it in her handbag, put her handbag in her lap and tried to settle again.

Jeanie's friends in that pub. The most awful thing, a forty-three-year-old woman doing drugs with a twenty-something girl. It made her think of the second-born in family number nine. So young, with so much promise. She'd looked a little dishevelled when she came to the hospital. Joy was suddenly worried about her. She was too unwell to probe at the time, but Camille was bruised; she looked vulnerable, scared even. She had just enough battery to text her:

Hi Camille, thanks so much for visiting me. Much better now. Hope you're doing okay? Mrs S x

Campsites were expensive. Joy wouldn't be able to afford such luxury very often. After her ablutions on Wednesday morning, she paid up and tidied her van for a day on the road. What road though? She didn't want to go too far. Jeanie might be in touch.

She turned the engine on to charge her phone. Camille still hadn't answered her message. She decided to go and check on her in person.

ᗱ

JE Collins, not JB – it seemed quite obvious looking at it now. Established 1895. She rang the bell three times before resorting to the knocker, which she banged as loudly as she could.

No response. Joy would have given up had she not heard music coming from the barred window at the side of the fortress. It was Camille's bedroom, the pottery room. She was home, or someone was.

'Yoo-hoo, are you there, hello?' she yelled from the side of the building. Nothing but music. It sounded happy-clappy.

'Camille, it's Mrs S,' she said, standing on her tiptoes but still unable to see through the window.

She walked around the back. The gate leading to the carpark wasn't locked, so she let herself into the courtyard, which was a bit of a disaster area. There were plastic bags everywhere. They were filled with men's clothing, knick-knacks and old newspapers. There was broken furniture. The bike shed was overflowing with stuff; its door swinging in the wind.

'Yoohoo!' she yelled, peering through the glass back door. The television was on in the living area. A true-crime show was playing. Someone was stabbing someone on the screen, again and again and again, stab, stab, stab. Joy did not understand why people watched this kind of thing. What was wrong with them?

'Hello!' she shouted to the person lying on the sofa in front of the telly. She wasn't sure who it was. All she could see were legs below the sofa. 'Camille, is that you? Camille?'

She bent down and had a closer look. No, no, it wasn't Camille's legs. There was an electronic bracelet on the ankle. It was Asha. But it wasn't two legs, it was just the one.

'Asha? Hello?'

The leg did not budge. She knocked on the glass door again. 'Asha, it's me.' It wasn't locked so she slid it open a bit. 'Asha, it's Mrs Salisbury.' The area had been scrubbed clean. Someone had been busy. It was gleaming.

'Asha?'

She did not sit up. Perhaps she was sleeping. Not wanting to scare her, Joy walked around to the front of the sofa slowly – 'Are you okay?' she said. 'It's just me, wondering if Camille is here. Asha?'

To her surprise, there was no-one on the sofa. She looked at the stone floor.

It wasn't a leg. It was half. It was a calf.

Joy screamed. Someone had severed Asha's leg at the knee. Someone had tied a belt around the middle of it, torniquet style, and bandaged the gristly, bloodless stump with a tea towel.

She lost her balance, nearly lost consciousness, wanted to throw up. It took her a moment to take stock and reach for her phone. It wasn't in her bag. It was charging in the van.

The religious music increased in volume and she heard Camille's voice. She was singing. Jesus Lord, something something something. Joy couldn't make it all out. Camille was alive. But she might be in danger. She might need help.

The lights up in the mezzanine were off. 'Penny, Andeep? Are you there?'

Nothing. No-one was up there. She was about to go out to the van to call the police when she saw a glass pipe on the kitchen bench. In a tin beside it was a small bag with crystals in it. Lord no, Ice.

She took the scalpel out of her bag and held it before her as she made her way towards the music and into the cavernous stone hall. Once crammed with upcycled homewares for sale, it was now empty bar the large dining table and a gathering of cleaning equipment that someone had recently used. The entire house was clean as a whistle and smelt of lemons. There was some mail on the table. Asha's bedroom door was open. There was no-one in there.

The door to Camille's room was closed. The music and singing she'd heard was coming from there.

'Camille.' She knocked. 'Camille? It's just me, it's Mrs S. Camille, are you all right, it's me.'

No answer.

The scalpel in her hand was shaking. She gripped it tighter.

She pushed the door open slowly, one inch at a time. The desk was under the high window, neat and tidy. The pottery wheel was in the middle. In the far corner, one of the enormous bluestones had been lifted up and was wedged against the wall. The hatch to the wine cellar. Camille must have discovered the secret of this old building.

Joy was trembling. How could Asha's leg have been severed? There might be a serial killer in the cellar. He might have had his dirty way with the girls and then murdered Asha and dismembered her. He might be forcing Camille to sing the song she's singing.

Joy started retreating from the room, one backward step at a time, the new-age hymn resounding from the hole in the corner. She steadied herself, holding the frame of the door, trying to breathe. She should run. She should go to the van and drive as fast as she can. She should pick up the axe by the door.

There was an axe by the door. Shiny clean, it was.

Then she heard Camille's voice again. Not singing, but chanting.

'*Rise, Asha, rise, I want to see your smiling eyes, I want to practise passes with you, I want to sing to daggy old songs and I want to dance, let's dance, Asha. Rise, rise, wake up wake up WAKE UP.*'

There was a floral notebook lying open on the desk. Joy glanced down at it:

> *…I think the meth is helping…*
> *…The answers just come at you…*
> *…I brought the axe back down … cut it right off…*
> *…If I stroke her face it gets warm…*
> *…Rise, Asha, rise, I want to see your beautiful smile…*

She flicked through previous entries, words and phrases jumping out at her:

> *…She broke my nose…*
> *…She shook me really hard…*
> *…Head butted me…*
> *…She bashed my back…*
> *…She pinched my arm…*
> *…Tug tug…*
> *…Stabbed my shoulder…*
> *…Get in the hole…*

Joy's heartbeat was matching the volume and rhythm of

the chanting that was echoing from downstairs. She put her hand on her heart, closed her eyes for a moment and then opened them again. She would not phone the police. She would not call the mum or the dad. She would be Nurse Joy, The Fixer, dressed in white, teeth perfect and polished, exactly the right tools at hand. Axe at her feet, scalpel in hand, she knelt at the edge of the opening. 'Camille,' she said loudly, 'it's Mrs S. Just me.'

The chanting stopped. Nothing for a while, then sobbing.

'Are you alone down there?' Joy asked.

The crying got louder. Joy couldn't hear anything else. It sounded like Camille was on her own.

'Is it just you down there?'

'No,' Camille's said in a small voice.

Joy edged back from the cellar opening. If Camille had someone else with her, she would not be able to help.

'Asha's here too,' Camille sobbed. 'It's just me and Asha.'

'No-one else?'

'No-one else.'

'If I come down will you hurt me?'

'Why would I hurt you?' Camille resumed her chanting. 'Asha, Asha, four, five, six, rise, please rise, I want to hear you play guitar, wake up now, wake, wake up Asha.'

'Okay, I'm coming down,' Joy said. She put the scalpel back in her handbag, secured the bag across her shoulder and edged her way down the ladder and into the cellar.

❦

Camille was crouched over her sister's mutilated and lifeless body; rubbing her face with her hands and counting: 'Thirty-eight, thirty-nine, forty...'

'Camille, it's me.'

She didn't stop what she was doing until she reached fifty, then she removed her hands from her sister's face and turned around and said: 'Her cheeks get warmer when I rub them.' She was kneeling on the dirt floor, her shorts and T-shirt smeared with blood, a bandage of sorts wrapped around her tummy. She had a wound on her shoulder with a small band-aid on it.

'Mrs S,' she said, reality slowly coating her face. 'We got into a really bad fight.' She looked at her sister, whose eyes were closed, her face grey. She had been dead for quite some time. Camille looked back at Joy. 'I don't think she's going to make it.' Her knees shook as if she was praying to Joy for the right response.

'No,' Joy said, looking at Asha's grey and stiff body. 'She's not, honey, she's gone.'

'She's gone?'

'She's gone.'

Camille crumpled into the dirt floor and reached out for Joy, grabbing her legs and sobbing.

'I saw your diary,' Joy said. 'I know what happened. I'm

sorry, I'm so sorry.' She wanted to hold the poor thing and cry with her, but there wasn't time for that now.

At the far end of the cellar, there was a huge, gaping hole. A mine shaft. No wonder the cellar had been closed off and kept secret. It wasn't in the deeds. Must have opened up after they built here. 'Where are your mum and dad?' Joy said.

Camille reached for her phone and swiped it onto the location app. 'Will you call them? I need to tell them. I need my dad. Oh my god, what have I done?'

Joy looked at the screen – Life360, it was called. There was a map showing that Camille was in Ballarat, that Penny was in Port Douglas. Andeep was in Sydney.

'Does anyone know about this place?' Joy asked.

'It's my hiding place,' Camille said.

'How far down does the mine go?'

'Dunno, miles.'

Joy put Camille's phone in her bag. 'Can you stand? Let's go upstairs.'

Joy followed Camille up the ladder, supporting her as she limped out of the bedroom and into the hall.

'Wait there a sec,' Joy said when they reached the door from the hall to the kitchen. She grabbed the bucket that was with the rest of the cleaning equipment, rushed over to the sofa and put Asha's severed calf inside, hiding it in the cupboard under the sink and covering it with a tea towel.

'Come,' she said, putting her arm around Camille again and helping her to the sofa.

She put a pillow under her head, a blanket over her. She turned off the true-crime show, flicked through the channels and settled on *Antiques Roadshow*.

'Here,' she said, offering her two Valium and a glass of water.

'I killed her.' Camille was rocking back and forth. 'Can you please call Dad? Call the police?'

'Let me get you sorted first.' Joy found some clean clothes for Camille and rummaged through the kitchen and bathroom cabinets until she had everything she needed.

'You know this is just a bit of skin, right?' she said, as she put antiseptic on her torn belly button and covered it with a bandage. 'Keep an eye on it, put Savlon on and change the bandage every day.'

Camille almost managed to nod.

'Your shoulder's not as bad as it looks.' Joy put a butterfly closure strip on the small wound. 'It'll heal on its own.'

She washed Camille with a warm wet flannel, changed her into a fresh long-sleeved T-shirt and loose jogging pants, and set about making toast and hot chocolate.

'Why won't you call the police?' Camille asked.

'Because.' Joy didn't want to say it out loud but she decided she needed to. 'Because you chopped off her leg with an axe after she died. And because you didn't call anyone for twenty-five hours. And because you're on meth.' She put the toast and hot chocolate on the coffee table beside Camille.

'I think I took too much,' Camille said.

'Promise me you will never take it again.'

'I'm not very good at promises.'

Ah, that was it, Camille was sipping the drink, taking a bite of the toast.

'Just call him, please,' Camille said.

Oh dear, Camille was now in the foetal position, rocking back and forth. 'What did I do, what did I do? I chopped off her leg. I chopped off her leg with an axe.'

Joy hugged her. It stopped the rocking.

'I promise, I promise. Never again,' Camille cried. 'She's dead, Asha's dead. I killed her.'

Joy held her shoulders, forced eye contact. 'Listen to me, you must never say that. It wasn't your fault. I should have listened to you. All of us should have listened to you. I'm really sorry. You have to remember that it was not your fault and never to say that. After I leave the police will come. You will say she ran off again. And when they can't find her you can be sad. You can cry with your mum and dad. Because she is missing. You can call me and you can cry with me. Because your sister is missing. Do you understand?'

'Where will you be?' she asked.

'Home,' said Joy.

eɔ

Every time she thought about what she must do with the leg, etc, she had to go to the bathroom and splash her face with water. With Camille semi-settled on the sofa, intermittently bursting into grief-stricken howls, the way Jeanie did after her dad died, she set about doing everything else. There was no hurry. Camille needed to be sane and sober when Joy left.

Fixer Joy would take all the time she needed. She would be thorough and methodical.

She scanned the mezzanine and was confident there was nothing there to cause suspicion.

She washed and dried Camille's dirty clothes.

She wiped Asha's phone clean and placed it on her bedside table.

She ripped Camille's diary, page by page, into tiny little pieces and placed them in hot water in the kitchen sink. As Camille rocked back and forth on the sofa, she watched the ink drain and the paper merge into little clumps of papier mâché, which she flushed, one by one, down the loo.

She checked that the hall was clean but not too tidy; that the fortuitous letters waiting for Asha were visible on the table – one from Ballarat Drug and Alcohol Counselling, another from Dr Fern Clancy at Ballarat Mental Health Services.

She checked that Camille's bedroom looked lived-in and as normal as a room with a pottery wheel in the centre can look.

She retrieved the original deeds she intended to return to Anne McLean from the van. She papier mâchéd and flushed them too.

She heated tomato soup.

She burned scented candles and opened windows to cover the smell of lemon bleach.

She fed Camille soup and more Valium.

She made coffee.

She checked Camille's phone to confirm that her parents were still in other states.

It was getting dark when Camille finally fell asleep. Joy forced herself to eat a small plate of soup and washed and dried the dishes.

There was no putting this off. She went outside to the van and returned with a comfortable but classy outfit, her makeup bag, a towel, and a small suitcase with her essentials, including her passport and her tartan photo album.

It was time.

Joy opened the cupboard under the sink and took the bucket out. It was heavy. The tea towel had fallen off. Necessary tools in her bag, she made her way to the cellar.

&

When Bertie used to slice people's mouths and gums, Joy had listened to music. She didn't mind the look of it, but she did not enjoy the sounds. She should have remembered this when she pressed her scalpel against the top of Asha's calf and sliced into it, cutting a line downwards, at about forty-five degrees, until almost reaching the ankle bracelet.

Before making the second incision, she attached her phone to the battery-operated speakers Camille had been using in the cellar and put her favourite song on repeat. It always put a spring in her step, this country song: a twang of joy, a skip of hope and harmony. She made a second cut from top to bottom, without nausea this time. There was now a V-shape incision on the leg, which she could peel off in order to slide the bracelet free. Using the scalpel, she sliced and chopped and peeled at it, turning the volume up a bit as she hit bone, depositing pieces of flesh into a plastic bag as she worked. When she was finished removing the large V of flesh, she slid the bracelet up and off. Done. She then sprayed and wiped the ankle bracelet and put it in her handbag. On the way to the airport, she would toss it out the window.

If she hadn't noticed the photo album beside Asha's body, Joy might have managed to remain calm. The cover had been ripped off, some of the pages had been torn out, the spirals twisted and loose. Happy family photos were a bad thing to look at right now. The wedding of Penny and

Andeep. Weddings, she should say. The first day of school for Asha Moloney-Singh. Camille's rabbit. Asha and Camille making a sandcastle in Portsea.

Joy turned the volume up even higher and walked over to the mine shaft, careful not to go too close. The earth was loose on its perimeter, she had to stand a few feet back. She threw the scalpel in the shaft, and then the glass pipe and the tin with its maniac-making crystals.

She thought about her wedding to Bertie at Avalon Castle. All very Melbourne elite, it was. There were a lot of dentists and none of Joy's family. Rosie couldn't afford to come back for it.

Music blaring, Joy retrieved the severed leg and the bag of flesh she had just sliced from it and threw them harder than she intended. They thumped against the side then dropped, out of earshot. The shaft did indeed seem to go down for miles.

She remembered Jeanie's first day at school. Her hair was in a ponytail. She'd said: 'Don't worry so much, Mum, I'm gonna be hunky-dory.'

Joy turned the music to maximum and began throwing everything in the cellar down the hole. The faux sheepskin gym mat cover, which was covered in clay and blood, the wine goon sacks, the candles, the bottles, the books, the bloody shirt she was wearing, the stained bra, the blood-soaked trousers, shoes, underpants, happy images coming at her with each throw: of new-born Jeanie, uni Jeanie, hockey Jeanie, florist Jeanie. By the time she heard a voice – was that a voice? Was someone calling her? – she had somehow managed to drag Asha's body to the edge of the mine shaft and was now completely naked on her back on the ground with her feet ahead of her, pushing it closer to the hole, kicking it closer – *Go … Get … Get away … Get down there … Get away … Get away from me* – until the corpse rolled and fell and disappeared and everything was quiet except her breathing and someone's voice – was that a voice?

'Mrs S?'

It was. Camille. That's right.

Joy was lying naked on her back. She was grazed and scratched and covered in dirt and in blood. She was breathing like a crazy person. Her song was blaring.

She shook herself, settled her breathing. She tried to stand but couldn't. She crawled to the bottom of the ladder, turned the music off and looked up: 'Sorry, could you run the shower for me please?'

Camille's face was peering down. She was pale, but she looked much better than she did before. 'You've got no clothes on. Are you okay?'

'I am,' said Joy. 'I'm coming up now. Run the shower for me like a good girl. On you go. I like it nice and hot.'

Joy scanned the cellar. She threw the speakers in the hole. There was nothing left now but the photo album and her handbag and her phone. She put her phone in her handbag, put her handbag over her bare shoulder and got to her feet. Then she made one final offering to the shaft – the Moloney-Singh photo album. She did half the sign of the cross, almost said a prayer, then made her way up the ladder.

ACKNOWLEDGEMENTS

Thanks to my amazing publishers for the encouragement and inspiration – Karen Sullivan, West Camel and everyone at Orenda Books in the UK, and Martin Hughes, Ruby Ashby-Orr and Laura Franks at Affirm in Australia. Also a huge shout to my agents, Philip Patterson at Marjcaq and Luke Speed with Curtis Brown. Lastly, to my writing buddy Lesley McDowell, who sat opposite me in cafés while I wrote this.